FALLOUT

Also by Garry Disher

The Dragon Man
Kittyhawk Down
Snapshot
Chain of Evidence
Blood Moon
Wyatt
Port Vila Blues
Whispering Death

FALLOUT

Garry Disher

Published by
Soho Press, Inc.
853 Broadway
New York, NY 10003

Library of Congress Cataloging-in-Publication Data

Disher, Garry.
Fallout / Garry Disher.
p. cm
ISBN 978-1-61695-103-0
eISBN 978-1-61695-104-7

1. Jewel thieves—Fiction. 2. Criminals—Australia—Fiction. 3. Boats
and boating—Australia—Fiction. 4. Australia—Fiction. I. Title.
PR9619.3.D56F35 2013
823'.914—dc23
2012049526

Printed in the United States of America

10 9 8 7 6 5 4 3 2 1

FALLOUT

By the fifth holdup the papers are calling him the bush bandit. An inspector of police, flat, inexpressive, resistant to the pull of the cameras, is less colorful: "We are looking for a male person who is armed and should be considered dangerous. His method of operation is essentially the same in every case. He targets a bank in a country town within an area covering west and southwestern Victoria and east and southeastern South Australia. He selects a quiet period when there are few if any customers, then menaces bank staff with a sawn-off shotgun, demanding cash from the tills. To date, we have no reports of an accomplice. I repeat, this person is armed. On no account should he be approached."

There are things that the inspector doesn't say. He doesn't say that the police are at a loss to pinpoint an operating base for the man. Given the area he moves in, the bush bandit might be holed up in Mount Gambier, Bordertown, Horsham, even somewhere up on the River Murray. Or he might be operating from Adelaide, even Melbourne.

The inspector doesn't say how effective the bandit is. First, the shotgun, its blunt snout, those twin black staring mouths. Everyone knows about shotguns, knows the massive damage they inflict at close range, the spread of the pellets, scattering and cutting like hornets. The dull gleam of the metal, the worn stock, the smell of gun oil. A shotgun spells gaping death, and so you are quiescent before it. You spread yourself out on the floor, you empty the till, you forget about being a hero.

Then there is the bandit himself. Witness descriptions tally for each of the five holdups. The man is tall and slender and he moves well. "Athletic," one bank teller said. "No wasted motions," said another. Other than that there is no clear description of the bush bandit. He varies his dress from job to job—a suit, jeans and a check shirt, zip-up windproof jacket and trousers, overalls, tracksuit. And something always to divert attention away from his face—glasses, sunglasses, cap, wide-brimmed Akubra, a Band-Aid strip.

He also speaks in fragments, so that bank staff are never able to get a clear fix on his voice: "Face down . . . fill the bag, please, no coins . . . foot off the alarm . . . don't move . . . don't follow." It's a quiet voice, that's all they can say. Calm, patient, understanding— these are some of the words the witnesses use. And young. They agree that he can't be more than about twenty-five.

Although they don't say it, the police believe that he's probably not a junkie. First-timers and junkies, they barge in screaming, pistol-whipping staff and customers, generally encouraging a condition of panic and instability that can tip over into hostages and spilt blood.

It's agreed that the man rides a big Ducati. No, a Kawasaki. Maybe a Honda. Big, anyway. Plenty of guts and very fast. Hard to track. On a bike like that he can be miles away before the alarm is raised. You can put up a chopper, send out a pursuit car, but all the bush bandit has to do is simply wheel off the road and under a gum tree or behind a windmill until the danger blows over.

Where does he store the bike? The police have no answer. Could be anywhere. Maybe their man has a dozen bikes stashed away, all around the country.

"One thing we do know," the inspector says, "one day he'll slip up. And we'll be there when it happens."

It was a wheat and wool town on a dusty plain. According to the local paper, the parade would pass down the main street between midday and half past twelve, turn left at the tractor dealership and wind its way on to the showgrounds next to the Elders-GM stockyards. This was the first anniversary of the Australia Day fire that had burnt out an area the size of Luxemburg and almost destroyed the town. In fact, the front actually licked at the edges of the high school, destroying a portable classsroom. Later the wind had changed, sweeping unseasonal rains in from the west, but not before Emergency Services personnel had lost one unit and two volunteer firemen. The shire president had wanted to run the parade on a Saturday, but feelings were still raw in the town and councillors voted for Australia Day itself, which this year fell on a Friday.

The man known as the bush bandit had never felt welling pride or sentiment for anything, but he knew how to read emotions. He walked down the main street, stopping to buy a newspaper, a half liter of milk, a packet of cigarettes that he would never smoke. A banner swayed in the wind, thanking the volunteer firemen. People were lining the footpaths, yarning and joking, cameras ready. Half of them were farmers and their families, and that's who the bush bandit was today, a pleasantly smiling farmer dressed in elastic-sided boots and a clean pressed work shirt and trousers. He wore a stained felt hat pushed back on his head. He looked work-worn and weary. He wasn't alone in wearing sunglasses. It's just that his were anachronistic, a flash narrow strip of mirrored glass across his eyes. They belonged on a rollerblading kid at St. Kilda or Bondi or Glenelg. If anyone thought about it, they thought the man had eccentric taste. Certainly it was the only thing memorable about his face.

He watched the parade trumpet past: police, firemen, ambulance crews, the two widows in the back seat of a squatter's black Mercedes. It was over in ten minutes, and the main street was deserted, the tail end of the spectators disappearing around the corner and away from the center of the town. There was only one bank, and the bandit walked into it at 12:25, removed his sawn-off shotgun from his bag of shopping, and announced that he was robbing the place.

There were no customers, only two tellers. One said, "Oh, no." The other froze. The bush bandit trained the twin bores of the shotgun on the one who'd spoken. He'd picked her as the likely source of trouble, so he said, "Face down. Not a sound."

He watched her sink to the floor. She stretched out awkwardly, one hand holding her skirt from riding up.

The other teller watched the gun swing around until it was fixed on her stomach. The bandit placed a chaff bag on the counter. "Fill it."

Friday. There would be more cash than usual, though not enough to make him rich. But that was a thought for the edge of his mind, a why-am-I-doing-these-pissy-jobs? thought for the dark hours.

He watched the teller, the shotgun now back on the woman on the floor. The meaning was clear: she gets it if you stuff me around.

At one point, the teller hesitated.

"Move it," the bandit said.

"Traveller's checks," she burst out. "You want them?"

Hundreds of checks, crisp, unsigned. The bush bandit could almost conjure up their new-paper-and-ink smell. He'd take them to Chaffey. Chaffey handled wills, property conveyancing, and sentence appeals in his front office; in his rear office he'd pay twenty cents in the dollar for anything the bush bandit turned up that wasn't cash or easily negotiable.

"Yes," the bush bandit told the teller.

When it was done, and both women were on the floor, he said, "Remain there, please. Five minutes."

One woman nodded. The talkative one said "Yes," but the man was already gone.

The motorbike was on the tray of a farm ute. He'd turned it into a farm bike with mud, dust, dents, a cracked headlamp. He drove the ute slowly away from the town, his elbow out the window, an irritating figure familiar to interstate coach drivers, truckies, and travelling salesmen, and soon he had faded into the landscape, faded from memory.

He ditched the ute on a dirt track and switched to the bike. This time it was a Honda and he'd stolen it in Preston. He ran into a storm, strong winds and driving rain, on the way back to the city, but by evening was in his balcony apartment, looking out over Southgate and the stretch of the Yarra River between the casino and Princes Bridge.

At eight o'clock he went out into the storm again and made his way to the casino to see if he could improve on the twelve thousand bucks he'd taken today. By morning he'd have the early edition of the *Herald Sun*, another bush bandit story for his scrapbook.

The bush bandit, that was his public name. Ray, or Raymond, those were the names his mother and father—both now dead—had called him. What Raymond wanted was simply to be called Wyatt. He liked the whiplash quality of the word.

But his uncle was called Wyatt.

Chapter 1

One hundred kilometers southeast of the city, the holdup man called Wyatt brought a crippled yacht in from the storm-tossed seas of Bass Strait to the calmer waters of Westernport Bay, bringing to an end a seven-day voyage from Port Vila. It was 4:15, almost dawn. Just five hours earlier, the bent police inspector called Springett had been washed overboard. Wyatt's only other passenger, the woman who had arrested Springett in Port Vila, was asleep on her bunk. Wyatt furled the torn sails and switched to the auxiliary diesel. The yacht burbled quietly between the red and green markers, following the channel to the little jetty on the Hastings foreshore. Liz Redding didn't stir, not even when Wyatt dropped anchor, bundled his clothing inside a waterproof jacket, and slipped over the side and away. She was too tired, too warm, too lost to the grains of Mogadon he'd fed her for that.

Wyatt dragged himself shivering from the water and wiped himself down with a handtowel from the yacht. He dressed rapidly in the shelter of a concrete retaining wall, occasionally poking his head above it, looking for fishermen, patrol cars, insomniacs. There were street lights behind a screen of foreshore trees; shire offices ghastly white in the sodium lamps; rows of slumbering small houses; a swimming pool and kiosk; a hut on the jetty that sold fish; and, to his left, a stiff forest of drydocked yacht masts behind a cyclone security fence.

What he wanted was a car.

If he left now, he would be in Melbourne by the time most people's alarm clocks were rattling them awake. If he were not so conspicuous—a stranger with wet hair appearing from the direction of the marina at the break of day—he'd take one of the town's taxis. Otherwise, there was the train, the local from Stony Point, connecting with the Melbourne express in Frankston, but that meant too many factors that he could not control, and which threatened to bring him unstuck—altered timetables, nosy ticket inspectors, faulty boom gates. Or he could hitchhike. But who would pick him up? Wyatt knew that the dark cast of his face, his fluid height, and shape and his materialization at the side of the road would spell prohibition and risk to any motorist.

And so his only option was to steal a car, one that would not be missed for the next couple of hours.

He ventured a short distance away from the little dock, into a region of humble side streets where the houses huddled together and the family car sat in the driveway or in the street outside it, straddling nature strip and gutter. But a dog barked. Wyatt backed out of there.

He couldn't see any service stations nearby. As he recalled it, they were mostly on the outskirts of Hastings. There are often cars parked outside service stations, keys on a hook somewhere inside.

He returned to the jetty. Wyatt had at first rejected the motley station wagons and utes parked there, fishermen's cars and rustbuckets all of them, with mismatched panels and doors and half a dozen registration stickers up and down the windscreens. He imagined their interiors, their snagging springs and crammed ashtrays and rolling UDL cans and faulty electrics. The Hastings police might turn a blind eye, allowing a local fisherman to drive between home and jetty and nowhere else, but Wyatt doubted that bald tires, rust, and cracked windscreens would pass in Melbourne.

But what choice did he have?

He could cut down on the risk, though, by driving to a place like Springvale, still well short of the city but a place where he wouldn't be looked at twice. Take a taxi from there.

Maybe three or four taxi journeys—angling north and south as he closed in on the city, so that anyone mapping his route would make little sense of it—and board a city tram at some big interchange like Kew Junction.

Wyatt checked his watch. 4:35. He hoped it was still too early for the first of the fishing boats to come in. He hoped its crew would have plenty to do when it did dock, leaving more time before one of them realized that his bomb was missing from the car park.

Wyatt went along the row of vehicles, testing drivers' doors and checking for keys left in the ignition. Most were unlocked—there was nothing worth stealing, after all—but no keys.

Then he checked behind bumper bars and inside wheel arches. He found plenty of rust, plenty of gritty mud. He also found a small metal container the size of a matchbox, held inside the wheel arch of a Valiant utility by a magnet.

There was nothing tight about the motor. It whirred freely and when it finally fired, Wyatt could hear piston slap and rattling tappets and smell the oily exhaust of poor combustion. The seat sagged, threatening backache and stiff neck and shoulders. Wyatt kept himself fit, but he was in his forties now and on the lookout for things like the size and shape of the seats he sat in and the beds he lay in.

But the headlights worked, the left angled higher than the right, and he found reverse without tearing a cog in the gearbox. The fuel gauge showed empty. Either that or it's stuffed, he thought. He couldn't risk filling it locally. He'd put some distance behind him first.

Wyatt cut across country toward Frankston. In the cool dawn light, fog appeared, hanging in the roadside depressions and above the creeks and dams, and hovering in thin streaks across the road, making him blink, as though to clear a film over his eyes. He remembered the fogs of the Peninsula from his recent past. There was a time when he'd strike fog on his way back from some smoking bank or payroll van. That was before he'd been forced to go on the run. That was a long time ago.

The engine coughed, surged, coughed again. The fuel gauge was working after all. Wyatt limped through the confusing roundabout in Somerville and into the Shell station on the Frankston road. The fisherman deserved a good turn: Wyatt filled the tank and poured a liter of oil down the throat of the clapped-out motor.

He abandoned the ute in a side street next to the level crossing in Springvale. He took a taxi to Westfield shopping center, a second to the taxi rank outside Myer in Chadstone, a third up to Northlands in Doncaster. He felt safer with each journey, as though he were shaking off the dogs and trackers of the past. The tram from Doncaster to the city was warm and quiet and full of early workers. If anyone looked at him it was incuriously.

There was a 24-hour café in Swanston Walk. Wyatt was bone-tired and hungry. They offered bottomless coffee and he downed three cups of it. He wanted something solid in his stomach and ordered muesli, scrambled eggs and wholemeal toast. He looked at his watch. Liz Redding should still be deeply asleep on her bunk aboard the yacht.

Revived, bouncy on his feet, he headed on foot along Little Lonsdale Street. At 8:30 he stepped into a call box at the Elizabeth Street corner and rang Heneker at Pacific Mutual Insurance.

In Wyatt's experience, all switchboard operators spoke with an upward inflection, as if framing every statement as a question, "I'm sorry? Mr. Heneker won't be in until nine?"

Wyatt hung up. He felt knots in his torso from his cooped-up days at sea. Thirty minutes to kill. He decided to walk, and as he stalked through the streets without seeing the shops, the cars, his fellow humans, he replayed his voyage across the Pacific with Liz Redding. But it all came down to one thing: he'd drugged her coffee and slipped away. He'd betrayed trust and desire. The fallout from something like that is often very simple: all bets are off.

At 9:05 he returned to the phone box and called the insurance company again. Heneker had the surging enthusiasm of his trade. "Heneker here, Mr.—"

He waited for a name. Wyatt didn't give him one. Instead, he said, "I've got the Asahi jewels."

He pictured the man, the white shirt and sombre suit and darting calculations. Heneker recovered quickly. "Shall we discuss where and when and how?"

"And how much," Wyatt said.

"How could I forget?" Heneker said.

Chapter 2

It wasn't strictly true that Wyatt had the Asahi jewels. He had one piece with him, a white gold necklace set with a dozen chunky emeralds, but the remaining pieces—rings, necklaces, brooches, pendants, tiaras—were still locked away in a concealed safe on board the yacht. Taken together, they were too bulky to cart around and too valuable to dump if he found himself in trouble. At the same time, he was not interested in fencing the jewels piecemeal or removing the stones and melting down the settings. To do that involved time and too many middlemen. Wyatt wanted to offload the Asahi Collection quickly, for a lump sum, the reward offered by the insurance company. The emerald necklace was simply his hook. It was the most eye-catching piece, promising more, yet also an easy thing to dump if the deal went sour.

Wyatt headed down Elizabeth Street, musing upon the twists and turns of his life. The Asahi Collection, touring Australia and New Zealand, had been stolen from a Japanese superstore in Melbourne. Wyatt wasn't the culprit—the actual raiders were policemen using security information supplied by Springett—but Liz Redding had suspected Wyatt. They'd both wound up in Port Vila, where Wyatt had discovered the hiding place of the Collection. He'd not revealed its location, not even when, on the voyage back, he and Liz had moved from being thief and thief-taker to being lovers.

Wyatt had almost been able to imagine a life with her. In the end, though, she was a cop, and Wyatt was a holdup man with a long history that would not withstand close scrutiny, and so he was on the run again.

The meeting place was an undercover car park on Lonsdale Street. He went in, climbing to the third level, where he prowled among the shadows. The ceiling felt very low, the air sluggish, fumy, and full of hard-to-place noises. The simplest sound was flat, hollow, booming.

He waited behind a concrete pillar. Heneker had described himself as "tall, a bit on the thin side, wearing a blue suit, carrying a *Time* magazine." When the insurance man finally appeared, Wyatt observed him for a couple of minutes. Heneker looked uneasy, the magazine held against his chest as though to ward off arrows. Wyatt supposed that he'd be nervous if he were in Heneker's shoes, and he stepped out into the weak light. "Mr. Heneker."

Heneker turned to him with relief. "Thought you weren't coming." He coughed. "What have you got for me?"

Wordlessly, Wyatt handed him the necklace. Heneker took it, wiped his sleeve across his face, and said, "A fake."

Wyatt faltered, just for a second. "Maybe the light's not bright enough for you."

Heneker looked around nervously, then said, his voice low and complicitous: "You don't understand. It's a copy. They're all copies, the entire collection."

Wyatt said nothing. He went onto his toes, ready to slip into the darkness.

"Good copies, mind you," Heneker said, getting back some of his nerve. "You'd need to be an expert. I mean, the settings are real enough, the white gold itself is worth a few bob, but the stones are all high-class fakes." He shrugged in the gloom. "The Asahi management got cold feet. Didn't want to pay the insurance premium for the real stones so we worked out a special deal for display copies. The collection toured right through New Zealand and Australia with no one the wiser."

"So why didn't you tell me to piss off on the phone?"

Heneker waved the necklace in the air. "These aren't cheap copies. Cost twenty grand to have them made up. We still want them back."

"How much?"

Heneker thought about it, swinging the necklace on his forefinger. "I'm authorized to offer five."

Wyatt smiled, like a shark, then laughed, a harsh bark in the slice of poisoned air between the concrete floors. "Five? Is that hundred or thousand?"

"Thousand," Heneker said, pocketing the necklace.

"Jesus Christ."

Wyatt turned away and began to merge with the shadows.

"You'd turn your back on five thousand bucks?"

No response. Wyatt continued to walk away. Heneker said, a little desperately now, playing for time: "I've got the five grand, here in my pocket."

Wyatt paused, came back, and said, with deadly calm, "The deal is this: you give me the five, I tell you where the other pieces are."

Heneker shook his head. "Pal, you must be desperate. First you bring me the entire Asahi Collection, then you get your five thousand."

The sounds when they came consisted of tire squeals on the up-ramp and the snap of shoe leather. At once Wyatt dropped to one knee and kicked out, hard into Heneker's groin and then into the shins of the man who had run in screaming: "Police! On the ground! Police! On the ground!"

Both men went down. Wyatt tackled the next cop. He heard a bone snap, heard a prolonged scream. And then in the noise and confusion, he ran.

Chapter 3

Raymond thought that if these people had any idea, *any idea*, that he was the bush bandit, they'd piss in their pants, spill their drinks, lose their hairpieces, tremble so hard they'd knock over their roulette chips. They *talked* hard and tough—mergers, windfall profits, takeovers, injunctions, lawsuits, union bashing—but it was all hot air, the men pink and soft, the women wasted by sunlamps and starvation diets to the consistency of old bootleather. Sometimes Raymond was tempted to pull a stunt with his sawn-off shotgun, risk gaol for the pleasure of wiping the greed and satisfaction from their faces.

They weren't all like that. Raymond played at a big-stakes roulette table in the far left corner of one of the upper-level salons. It was a table that attracted your vulgarians, sure, but it also attracted the occasional cool, unblinking Asian gambler, who'd make and lose a fortune without feeling that he had to advertise it to the world, the occasional professional from Europe or the States, and the occasional middle-aged business type who'd looked after his health and didn't make a fuss about how big he was.

This particular roulette wheel brought luck to Raymond. Or rather, he knew it would be unlucky to switch to one of the other tables. On average, he was ahead—win twelve grand one night, lose eight or nine the next. A week ago he'd won twenty-five. Two nights later he was down thirty. It all meant that he lived a good life but there wasn't much hard cash in his pocket. Tonight he was behind, most of the cash from the bank raid gone down the drain.

It was a relative term, "losing." Raymond never had a sense of falling behind, not when he could simply go out and pull another job to top up his reserves. And there were the other positives: the women, the covetous glances, the contacts like Chaffey—whom he'd met playing craps—and the intoxicating dreamland of tuxedos, crisp white cotton, strapless dresses, his own lean jaw and sensitive hands in the muted 24-hours-a-day light.

A number of regulars played this table. Others liked to watch. Raymond was on nodding terms with all of them, but in the past couple of weeks he'd found himself drawn to the company of a man called Brian Vallance and Vallance's girlfriend, Allie Roden.

He watched them now as he stacked his chips. Vallance was quick and compact looking, with olive skin and a closely trimmed grey beard on his neat chin. He had a healthy outdoors look, but Raymond wasn't sure that he liked Vallance. There was a sulkiness close to the surface, the mouth was too mean, Vallance's body language too buttoned-down. Vallance was about fifty, and that put him about twenty-five years older than the girlfriend.

Now there was a sight for sore eyes. Allie Roden had thick auburn hair like flames around a finely boned face, a kind of slow, deep consuming fire in her green eyes, white skin, a beautiful shape, and a readiness to toss back her head and laugh aloud. When she did that, Raymond wanted to bite her throat.

She came around the table while the croupier was making ready for the next spin of the wheel. Raymond felt her hand touch his wrist briefly, smelt her—a hint of plain soap and talc—as her lips brushed his ear and she murmured, "Let's have a drink when you're ready."

Raymond didn't take his eyes away from the croupier's hands. He nodded, sensed Allie step back, her fingers brushing his shoulder. When next he looked, she was standing behind Vallance. They both looked keenly at him and Vallance flashed a grin.

Raymond played on, losing, winning, pushing chips onto the board, pulling them toward him. Then he won five grand on one play, and that was his signal to stop and have a drink with Vallance and Vallance's woman. He raised an eyebrow, inclined his head, and left the table.

"That was a daring play," Allie said, coming around the table and winding her slim hand into the crook of his arm.

He liked the bouncy quality of her affection and generosity. No one minded, least of all Vallance. He wasn't possessive or jealous. Raymond couldn't see what she saw in him, though. There was the age factor, the hint of weakness in the man, her own energy and enthusiasm. She deserved better.

"You win some, you lose some," Raymond said.

Vallance, at his other elbow as they walked to a secluded table in the lounge, said, "You win more often than you lose, Ray. I've been watching. It's a real education. You're careful. You're not a man to throw his money away."

Raymond played that coolly. He wasn't about to tell Vallance that he'd borrowed ten grand from his fence, the lawyer Chaffey, meaning that the five grand he'd just won was no longer his. With any luck, Chaffey would allow him a further five for the traveller's checks and wipe out the debt completely.

They sat down, ordered champagne to celebrate. The talk circled around money and expert and inexpert gambling play. It emerged that Raymond was independently wealthy, from a good family, and gambled because he liked it. "I can take it or leave it, though," he said. He was no mug. Nothing desperate or pathetic about Raymond Wyatt.

They talked and ordered a bottle, Dom Perignon, Raymond forking out the best part of two hundred bucks for it. And then, unmistakably, Allie's shoeless foot scratched his ankle, and he felt the hot press of her thigh as she reached across him for the bottle. For the first time, Raymond thought that with a bit of skilful maneuvering on his part he could extricate her from Vallance.

They relaxed, and into the warm glow of the endless night—it could have been a bright spring day outside for all Raymond knew or cared—Vallance slid a tin of shoe polish across the table. "Take a gander inside that, young Raymond."

The tin felt hefty in Raymond's hand. If it was shoe polish, it was very dense. He shook the tin and something shifted within it, a sense of heaviness and solidity transmitting itself to his fingers.

"Go on, it won't blow up on you."

Raymond pressed where it said press and the lid popped open. He lifted it off, stared in, and saw what accounted for the heaviness and the bulk.

"Gold guinea, dated seventeen ninety-nine," Vallance said. "Silver florin, too worn by saltwater corrosion to establish the date but roughly the same vintage. Spanish silver dollar, dated eighteen ten, and the one with the hole in it is a holey dollar, scarce as hen's teeth."

He paused. "I've got an airlines bag full of similar stuff at home. What's more, I'm the only man alive who knows where the rest is buried."

Something stirred in Raymond, a kind of hunger, a hazy dream of adventure on the high seas, flintlock pistols, and treasure chests. He looked up at Vallance uncomprehendingly.

"Why are you showing me?"

"You strike me as a man who knows how to keep his trap shut."

"Maybe."

"I won't bullshit you—you're in a position to help me and Allie."

"You're the one with the story to tell," Raymond said patiently.

He felt Allie's foot again. At the same time, she leaned over and slid an arm around Vallance. Raymond watched the man melt a little and rub his jaw over her skull. She said, "Brian used to chart wrecks for a living."

Vallance said defiantly, "Until a year ago, Ray, I worked for the Maritime Heritage Unit. Our job was to locate wrecks from old documents, chart and excavate known wrecks, and safeguard others from scavengers. We even had a cop assigned to us full-time. Part of her job was checking Sotheby's and Christie's on the lookout for looted artifacts."

Raymond waited.

A flush of anger filled Vallance's lined face. "I was accused of stealing artifacts that hadn't yet been catalogued. Accused of selling to a private buyer. It was all bullshit. They couldn't prove anything, but I'd had enough so I quit rather than work for those bastards again."

Sure you did, Raymond thought. *You fucked up and almost got caught.* It pleased him oddly to be listening to this desperado's story, almost as if Vallance could only be trusted because he was crooked.

He saw Allie pat Vallance's arm. In the dim light her features were soft and attentive. Raymond felt himself burning for her. He absently touched a finger to the coin with the hole in it.

"Tell you what, Ray," Vallance said. "That Spanish dollar is yours, whether you help us out or not. It's rated very fine, worth around a hundred and seventy-five bucks. All I want you to do at this stage is listen, no obligation to invest."

"Invest?"

"Fifty grand could get you five million," Vallance said.

Chapter 4

The lawyer called Chaffey eased forward in his chair, the heat of effort rising on his broad, soft, clean, unhealthy face. He placed both hands on his desk and push-straightened his legs. Now he towered giddily against the window and, as he buttoned the vast folds of his suit coat together and prepared to show Denise Meickle out of his office, he glanced down upon the plane trees and tram tracks of St. Kilda Road, the flashing chrome and foreshortened pedestrians, the park benches and rollerblading kids, trying to muster unfelt confidence into his voice.

"Leave it with me."

The Meickle woman was a sorry-looking creature, small, mousy, belligerent. She was in love with a client of Chaffey's, a holdup man and killer called Tony Steer, who was being held in the city watchhouse. He was about to be transferred to somewhere more permanent and Denise Meickle wanted Chaffey's help in springing him from gaol.

"First," she said, reluctant to leave, though she'd been with him for an hour now and gone over everything a dozen times, "you'll have to make sure he's transferred to the remand center in Sunshine. Sometimes they're remanded in Pentridge, but we'll never spring him from there."

Chaffey had doubts that Steer could be sprung from the remand center, let alone Pentridge. "Leave it with me," he said again.

Meickle had been a prison psychologist attached to the gaol in Ararat when she first befriended Steer. Given the complex nature of a gaol environment, in which prison staff have to offer both welfare and custodial roles, it wasn't hard for someone like Meickle to blur or confuse these roles. It was especially hard for custodial staff who might find themselves comforting a bereaved prisoner one minute and strip-searching him the next. As a psychologist, Meickle hadn't had that kind of relationship with Steer, but the intimacy and role confusion were no less compelling. "We'll get your man out," Chaffey said.

She didn't want to go. She numbered her fingers, so that Chaffey would get it straight. "So this is the deal. New Zealand passports for both of us, a boat out of the country, and someone to help me spring Tony. For that we pay you fifty thousand dollars. Find someone good, someone who can drive and keep his nerve. Pay him out of your cut." She poked Chaffey's huge midriff. "Don't rip us off. We'll find you if you do."

Chaffey nodded his massive head. He was Tony Steer's lawyer and minded Steer's money for him. He had more sense than to rob the man. Steer was bad news, a hard, fit man of flashing confidence and intelligence. Chaffey thought of the legions of women who befriended male prisoners. Lonely women, many of them, fired by good works, God or pity. Some of them married killers, waited for them to get out, and got killed for their pains. Maybe that's what awaited Denise Meickle.

He ushered her to the door. "I'll get onto it straight away. The passports, the boat, no drama there. Finding a good man will require a bit of thought."

"No junkies. No mugs. No one with form."

"Like I said, I'll get straight onto it."

"He goes to trial in two weeks' time. We haven't got much time."

When Meickle was gone, Chaffey ran through a mental checklist of names. None looked promising: dead, in gaol, feeding a habit or too narrow in their fields of expertise.

The phone rang.

"Chafe? Raymond here. How are you placed today?"

Here was someone he hadn't thought of. "Raymond, old son." Chaffey checked his watch. "Meet you in thirty?"

"Usual place. I've got some paper for you."

That could mean anything: bonds, numbered sequences of bills, checks. "See you then," Chaffey said, cutting Raymond off before he compromised both of them on the line.

In the outer office he said, "Back in an hour."

"But you've got appointments."

"Back in ninety minutes," Chaffey said.

He put one foot after the other down the corridor. The lift gulped and clanked, dropping seven storeys with Chaffey braced, legs apart, at the midpoint of the floor, as though he were riding it to the ground. It hit the bottom, recovered, and Chaffey shouldered through the foyer to the street.

The "usual place" was a booth in Bourke Street Mall that dispensed cheap theatre and concert tickets. Cursing, for there were no taxis in sight, Chaffey propelled himself toward the nearest tram stop.

Five minutes later he was strap hanging in a draughty rattletrap along Swanston Street. It claimed to have the University as its destination, but that didn't mean it wouldn't reverse direction shortly or veer into Victoria Street. The seats looked minute and insupportable to Chaffey. He didn't trust them, or the conductor, or the other passengers. The students among them flashed their white teeth and clawed great arcs of gleaming hair away from their eyes as they spoke loudly, sub-literately, to one another. Otherwise there were pensioners, stunned and dazed, and women in suits with flying shoulders, snapping gum in their jaws.

Chaffey stood with his feet apart and tried to brace his solid legs in a counter-rhythm to the tram. His reflection in the glass revealed his bulk, a button nose, red lips, long pale lashes, and damp acres of pink skin. It didn't reveal his vicious glee, for he was dreaming of Raymond Wyatt saying that he would help Denise Meickle spring Tony Steer out of remand.

Chaffey alighted at Bourke Street, stepping down from the tram in careful stages, his movements as slow and ponderous as he could make them, thereby doing his bit to fuck up the timetable. Traffic braked for him as he heaved toward the footpath.

He found himself face to face with the three bronze statues bolted to the footpath. They were tall, rubbery-looking caricatures of businessmen, their faces a little desperate in the swirling toxins. They were also painfully thin and Chaffey, spotting a swagger of body builders outside a nearby Sports Barn, wrapped his big arm around one of the statues and grinned. The body builders, all violet shellsuits and body hair, stopped chewing and posturing, looking about for the insult.

Chaffey steered a straight course down the mall. He did not have to dodge or weave or break his stride. As he walked his eyes darted left and right, hoping that Raymond was still unknown to the law.

Even so, Chaffey had to admit that the mall was a good place to meet. The center mile of the city was as useful as a sieve to anyone trying to seal it off. It was made up of lanes and alleys and back streets, all leading away from the center. Raymond could easily slip away, or hole up *inside* the center mile, up in some men's lavatory along a dim corridor on the second or third floor of a seedy side-street building where the tenants gave singing lessons, altered suits, and made dentures.

Chaffey reached the ticket booth. He spent a few minutes circling it, reading the posters, then he stood facing up the mall toward Parliament House, his hands seeking purchase on his soft hips.

Raymond materialized at Chaffey's shoulder, tall and fluid-looking in a tuxedo, very calm and still, yet clearly prepared to vanish into the shopping crowds if he felt threatened. "Chafe, old son."

Chaffey beamed, his mind ticking over. Raymond was a long streak of quiet menace to look at, a man with a hard, cautious mind. Most thieves that Chaffey dealt with were full of doubt and spite and contradictions, their minds tripping them up every minute of the day. Here was a man who registered, analyzed, then acted, all of it manifested in extreme alertness.

He did like to play the tables, though. "What's with the tux?"

Raymond grinned. "Just finished an all-night session."

"Win?"

"Got your five grand, plus the paper I was talking about."

"Not here. Let's go."

They walked up Bourke Street to Chaffey's club, on the corner of King Street. It was a cloaked and sombre warren of private rooms and alcoves, where lawyers met clients and other lawyers. It was a place where Chaffey's conversation with Raymond would go unremarked, even if it was overheard.

Raymond stretched his long legs. "In the briefcase."

Chaffey opened it. Traveller's checks, crisp and new, and a roll of $100 bills. "Twenty cents in the dollar," he said.

Raymond shifted in his chair. The leather, old and cracked and friable, creaked under him. "I was hoping the five grand plus the paper would cancel the ten I owe you."

Chaffey closed the briefcase. He gave a short laugh. "Fair enough, but I think you owe me in *spirit*, if nothing else. I can put two jobs your way, one pays fifteen grand, the other a hundred."

Raymond watched him carefully. "Hundred grand? What do I have to do for that?"

"I've got a client prepared to pay a hundred thousand dollars for a collection of paintings."

"Where are these paintings?"

"At present they're hanging in the University of Technology in West Heidelberg," Chaffey said.

For the next ten minutes, he described the job, explaining how lucrative art theft was. "This job," he concluded, "will be a pushover. No alarms, no cameras."

Raymond stroked his bony jaw. "I don't know. What do I know about art? I'd need a partner, someone who knows that kind of thing." He paused. "What's the other job?"

Chaffey told him about Steer and Denise and the remand center. "You get fifteen grand—up front, how's that for a sweetener? All you have to do it spring Steer, hole up with him and his girlfriend for a couple of days, then deliver them both to a freighter anchored off Lakes Entrance."

Raymond turned a little sulky then. It spoilt his looks. "Spring some guy from remand? Bit downmarket isn't it?"

Chaffey shrugged. "Quick, easy money. All you have to do is drive a car and babysit for a few days."

"I'll think about it."

"You do that," Chaffey said.

Raymond stiffened, cocked his head. "Sirens. Hear them?"

"Just so long as they haven't come for you, old son," Chaffey said.

Chapter 5

Wyatt ran and the cops ran, Wyatt's shoes snickering minutely across the prefabricated concrete levels of the parking station. The cops were noisier, shouting, grunting with exertion, their footwear heavy and booming. As he ran, Wyatt took a baseball cap from the pocket of his jacket, threw the jacket under a parked car and rolled the sleeves of his shirt to the elbows. It was not much, but a little was often all he needed.

Wyatt reasoned it through as he ran. If Heneker had warned the cops, then they'd have arranged a trap at the parking station. Instead, they arrived late, indicating that they'd followed Heneker without foreknowledge of the actual meeting place.

There was only one explanation: Liz Redding had shaken off the effects of the Mogadon and alerted the police in Melbourne to tail Heneker. And that meant she'd come to suspect that Wyatt had the jewels after all and wasn't simply making a run for it. She was a cop, and Wyatt was Wyatt, so it was only natural that she'd suspect further treachery beyond the obvious and assume that he'd attempt to strike a deal with the insurance company.

Wyatt ran to the top level, to a door marked EXIT. He pushed through and found himself in a department store cafeteria.

Better cover than he'd hoped for. The chunky white crockery smacked onto plastic trays, the stainless steel cutlery rattled in serving bins, hot quiche steamed behind glass, the chrome rails gleamed. He was swept into a clamorous queue at the servery. Morning tea. He lifted an abandoned *Herald Sun* from a corner table, loaded two pastries and black tea onto his tray, and went looking for someone who could turn him into a law-abiding citizen.

All of the tables were occupied and most of the chairs. Wyatt's eyes passed over the tables where he'd stand out or invite irritation. He didn't want elderly couples, friends enjoying coffee together, solitary eaters or office workers snatching a break from work.

There, at the center of the crammed area of tables—a woman with a pram and two fractious children. Wyatt edged through to the unoccupied chair, said, "May I?" and unloaded his tray and opened his newspaper. The woman glanced at him tiredly and went back to juggling the competing needs of the baby and the two older children. The children ignored her. They were squabbling over a date scone.

"Here," Wyatt said. He nudged his pastries across the little table. "I haven't touched these. I don't really want them."

The woman flashed him a cautious smile. Deciding that he wasn't a threat, she said, "Say thank you to the nice man."

The children stared at him, looked down, muttered aggrievedly.

"You're welcome," Wyatt said.

He scanned the newspaper. He'd been living in Tasmania before events had taken him to Vanuatu, and was out of touch. A holdup man called the bush bandit had been hitting banks in country towns. The reporter used words like "cool" and "unhurried" and "well-planned" to describe the man and his actions. Wyatt wondered who it was. There was a time when he would have known something like that. Whoever the man was, he was part of a dying breed. Junkies had got into the game now. They were vicious and desperate and prone to taking stupid risks.

Wyatt became aware of a shift in the atmosphere. Police, at least four of them, two in uniform, taking care not to alarm anyone but still scanning the cafeteria. Their heat and eagerness and frustration were palpable. He said to the children, "What do you recommend? Should I go and see the new James Bond film?"

They kneeled on their chairs, craning to see his finger on the cinema ads. And their mother looked, welcoming the diversion. If you didn't know it, Wyatt and the woman and her children were a family in town for the day—shopping, morning tea, a film for the kids before they went home.

A ripple passed across the room and then it was gone, replaced by crockery smack again, laughter, complaints: the sounds of the city feeding itself. Wyatt got the woman to talk. He did that by asking her questions about her children. After a while she began to notice him, faintly longing, faintly wary. She colored a little, inclined her body toward him, switched from talking about her children to talking about herself. She had no hope or expectation of anything, just grateful that someone should take an interest.

In a little while, the cops came back, as Wyatt had supposed they would. They found the cafeteria essentially unchanged. There were husbands and fathers among the diners and one of them was Wyatt. They faded away again.

Wyatt got to his feet, showing reluctance. "Afraid I have to go."

"Yes."

He took the escalators to the bargain basement, alert for

trained moves and involuntary gestures, anything that promised trouble—hands curling near pockets, eyes flicking with recognition, mouths turned away to lapel microphones or radios. He was in a crowded space but moved through it as though along a deserted street, jettisoning the clutter in his mind and limbering his body for the moment he'd need to think and act faster than those who were going up against him.

He saw cops on the way down. They didn't see him. They were abandoning the search. The hard scrutiny had gone out of their faces.

At the bottom he filled two logoed shopping bags with cheap, bulky kitchen goods. Bit by bit he was building up his credibility. On the way out he bought sunglasses and a straw hat. On the streets of the city he was one among the thronging thousands.

The city offered trains, buses, and planes that would take him out of the state, but he knew that the police would be watching the major terminals. He had to take a less direct and obvious route out. There were flights across Bass Strait from Tyabb, near Westernport Bay. Westernport was also where all this had started, so no one would be looking for him there.

He walked to Flinders Street station, stopping from time to time to listen to the spruikers spilling onto the footpath outside the discount stores. Wyatt had no interest in the cheap and useless bargains. He was looking for gestures and movements again.

He took the express to Frankston. Thirty minutes later he was on the train to Westernport Bay. When he got out at Hastings it was late morning and he did not look out of place among the handful of other shoppers returning from the city.

Wyatt wandered down the main street. There was an opportunity shop opposite the new library. He went in, stacked the kitchenware on the counter, nodded, and went out again, toward the jetty.

As Wyatt saw it, Liz Redding would be questioning Heneker by now. It wouldn't occur to her that the jewels were still on the yacht. It was a long shot, but maybe they hadn't got around to impounding it yet. Maybe it still sat at anchor.

A long shot. What Wyatt found was the yacht tied to a jetty inside the marina with a yellow crime-scene tape all around it.

He walked back up the main street. At the library door he veered to avoid colliding with one of the librarians. She was young, fair, ready to smile, and glanced at him as he edged past her into the foyer and put coins in the public phone. Wyatt asked about flights to King Island. There was one at 4 P.M. He booked a seat, looked at his watch, and saw that he had four hours to kill.

Chapter 6

Liz Redding hurried from the staff room at the police complex, coffee slopping over her fingers. They had Heneker in the interview room.

There were two men with him: her superintendent, Montgomery, looking slightly out of his depth, and Gosse, her new inspector. She didn't like Gosse. She'd never seen him smile; he reduced the civilian typists and filing clerks to tears three or four times a week; he'd look past you as though you were nothing to him while he spoke to you.

Montgomery climbed to his feet. "Come in, Sergeant Redding."

Gosse frowned, as though to argue, but then he shrugged and turned away from her. *It's already started,* Liz thought. *Gosse will freeze me out and soon have Montgomery doing it too.*

The room was small and bare. Liz glanced at Heneker. He'd been the last person to see or speak to Wyatt, and she felt a surprising need to be alone with him, ask him if Wyatt looked okay, even though Wyatt had doped her coffee last night and run from her. She'd awoken feeling thick in the head but had known at once what had happened. She'd alerted Montgomery from a pay phone in Hastings, and Montgomery had alerted the insurance company.

Heneker looked nondescript, dishevelled by the struggle in the undercover car park. He brushed grit from the knees of his trousers, dabbed a damp handkerchief at an oil stain. His tie was crooked, his suit coat crumpled, the collar turned up.

"What more can I tell you?" he said, looking at Gosse.

Liz mentally framed a question, but suddenly was racked with yawns. They threatened to lay her across the table.

"Sergeant Redding?"

She gulped her coffee. "I'm fine, sir."

"Carry on, Inspector."

"Mr. Heneker—"

He looked up. "This being taped? I want a lawyer."

"You're not under arrest, for God's sake. A few more questions—"

"Then I can go home?"

"Of course," Liz said.

Gosse twisted his mouth at the interruption and threw down his pen.

Heneker took advantage of it. He put his head on one side and narrowed his eyes at Liz. "If I may say so, you don't look a hundred percent."

A basic rule was: never let the bastards start to question *you*. Liz said, "Let's start from the beginning. You got a phone call? A visit?"

"Phone call."

"After we contacted you?"

"Yes."

Gosse picked up his pen again. His knuckles were white around the barrel. This was *his* show. "A man? Did he give his name?"

"Nope."

"Didn't recognize his voice?"

"Nope."

"When you saw him, did you recognize him?"

"Nope."

Montgomery's chair creaked. Like a kindly uncle he said, "Your firm ever encountered a man with the name of Wyatt before? He does this sort of thing, commits a robbery, negotiates a reward from the insurance company."

Neither Liz nor Gosse could bring themselves to look at Montgomery. Montgomery would be better off back in Traffic, from whence he'd come. One, he'd given Heneker a name, if Heneker didn't already have it. Two, Heneker could start doing his own checking now. Three, by butting in he'd eased what little tension she and Gosse had been able to generate in the room, meaning they'd have to start all over again. It didn't seem that Heneker had anything to hide, but it wouldn't be the first time that a burglar and an insurance agent had worked hand in hand.

Heneker shrugged. "Wyatt? Was that his name? Can't say I know it."

Gosse said, "Let's go back to the phone call. What did the caller say?"

"Wyatt? He—"

"Not necessarily Wyatt," Montgomery said. "There could be others."

Gosse threw down his pen again. Heneker's eyes opened wide. "You mean there's a gang?"

"Just tell us what the caller said."

"He said straight out that he had the Asahi Collection."

"And?"

"Well, naturally my ears pricked up. I mean, there was hell to pay when those stones got lifted. Phone calls from Japan all hours of the night and day. Quiet word from the Japanese consul. You name it, I had to take it."

"Your company wanted the stones back."

"Sure."

"You told the caller that you'd meet him?"

"Yep."

"Did you suggest the parking station?"

Heneker was getting agitated. "He did. You know all this."

"So you'd never seen this man before?"

"Never. I told you that."

Liz leaned forward. "What did he say?"

"Wasn't much of a talker."

She knew the truth of that. She'd spent seven days with Wyatt and in that time had learnt almost nothing about him. His *body* had told her things, communicating desire, even affection and regard, and he'd relaxed enough to smile readily, if tiredly, but he had no small talk and he imparted no secrets, even though he was full of them. Time—a lot of it—might have helped. Time, and stepping over the line. What would it be like, leading his risky life with him? Would he have stepped over the line for her? She'd never know now.

"He must have said something to you. Didn't he offer proof that he had the stones, for example? Didn't he ask how much the reward would be?"

"Nope."

Gosse snarled, "He was observed handing you something, Mr. Heneker."

Heneker shifted in his chair. He reached inside his coat pocket. "All right, all right, he gave me this."

A necklace spilled onto the table. For a moment they were silent in the face of the soft glow, the winking hard stones.

Liz said, "You're not a trustworthy man, are you, Mr. Heneker? Do your superiors know that?"

"I get results."

"What were you going to do with the necklace? Sell it?"

Montgomery looked pained. "Mr. Heneker is not suspected or accused of anything, Sergeant Redding. What we have to focus on is this man Wyatt."

"Yes, sir."

Gosse leaned forward. "Did he have the other pieces with him?"

Heneker shook his head. "Didn't see them."

"Did he tell you where you could find them?"

"Nope."

"You didn't warn him?"

"Inspector Gosse," Montgomery began. "Mr. Heneker is—"

Gosse ignored him. "You didn't arrange to meet this man later?"

Heneker was outraged. "What do you take me for? You called and said he might contact me. He did, so I let you know. I've done my bit. If a dozen of you are not capable of catching one man, then that's your problem, not mine."

"All right, all right, Mr. Heneker. I'm sure Inspector Gosse doesn't mean any offense. Is there anything else you can tell us about the man? He didn't say where he was staying? Didn't give you a number to call? Didn't mention any names. Nothing like that?"

"Not a thing."

"Then you may go."

"What about the necklace?"

"We'll need to hang on to it for the time being," Gosse said, "pending further investigation."

Heneker shuffled out, scowling, putting plenty of outrage into the tilt of his head. Heneker smelt wrong. Liz didn't know how, but knew that he'd held something back, some fiddle.

She was lost to these thoughts and didn't register the hard stares of Gosse and even Montgomery until it was too late. Gosse said, "Nice tan, Liz."

Liz stiffened. *Here it comes,* she thought.

"So, you decided to go to Vanuatu and arrest Inspector Springett."

"Yes."

"Yes, *sir,*" Gosse said.

Liz shrugged.

"An unauthorized trip to a country over which the Victoria Police have no jurisdiction. You came back with Springett and this man Wyatt, only Springett drowned in yesterday's storm and Wyatt gave you the slip, the Asahi jewels in his pocket. Correct, so far?"

"Sir, you have to take into account—"

"I hope to God the press don't get wind of this, Sergeant," said Montgomery. "They'd have a field day."

Gosse said irritably, "Sergeant, you can understand that we have a problem with your story. The jewels. Your relationship with this Wyatt character, Springett's convenient death."

Liz struggled against the fog in her head. There was a blowfly buzzing against the glass above the chair in which Heneker had been sitting. Why had Wyatt thought it necessary to drug her? Why had he run? Such contempt and calculation after their seven days together. She felt incomplete and grubby, as if she'd had no say at all in their . . . encounter. As if he'd had all the power. And he'd had the Asahi jewels all along.

She felt muddled and dreamy. Montgomery and Gosse talked around her, talked about charging her, pending suspension and an inquiry. Liz let them talk.

She'd been seven days on the open sea in the stolen yacht before she saw the change in Wyatt. It had happened as they neared the eastern seaboard. She'd been expecting it. He was a holdup man, after all. Their days together in the briny air and mild sun were simply a respite from the running that was mostly his life and the hunting that was mostly hers. Then the first land birds and rusty coastal freighters had appeared to remind her that she had a job to do, just as she supposed Wyatt was reminded that he had a fortune in jewels in his possession and a cop for a travelling companion.

God, was it only yesterday afternoon? She remembered that he had checked the compass bearing, referred to the chart, made a slight adjustment to the wheel. Rough seas had been forecast, and for Liz that was the precipitating factor.

She'd stood at his elbow, staring down at the chart, then used her finger to trace the coastline of Victoria from Wilsons Promontory to the rip at Port Philip Heads, and up into the bay toward Port Melbourne. "How big a storm?" she'd asked.

"I wouldn't want to be tossing about in it."

"So what do we do?"

"Put in somewhere until it blows over."

"Where?"

She loved his hands. Wyatt had pointed with a finger as slender and worn as a twig weathered by the wind and the rain. "Westernport marina at Hastings. We can be moored there by about four o'clock in the morning."

Liz remembered saying, to gauge his reaction: "I could call CIB detectives to come down and collect us in Hastings. No need to wait for the storm to blow itself out."

Wyatt had said nothing, his face settling into an impassivity that he wore like a familiar shoe. He could not be read, and that annoyed her.

"Wyatt? We have to talk about this."

But he stared out at the sea, sombre and cryptic, a hard alertness under it. Impatiently she said, "Do you want to spend the rest of your life running and hiding? I'll bring you in. I doubt if you'll do any gaol time."

She squirmed now, remembering this. He must have thought her either naive or devious. But she'd gone on, pestering, cajoling. "Your testimony will help me clear everything up."

"I had nothing to do with Springett or his operation."

"Not directly, maybe, but—"

"So I can't help you."

"You mean you won't help me."

"I won't help you put me in gaol, certainly."

A wave had heaved out of nowhere and they breasted it, tilted, hung there in space, and returned with a crash to the horizontal. Liz had felt her teeth snap together. Wyatt fought the wheel until they were pitching and butting through the surface chop again. They could see coastal towns in the muted light of the approaching dusk. Darkness fell rapidly after that; the sea grew rougher; their running lights burned in the seaspray.

Then the yacht yawed violently. When it was stable, Wyatt said, "You'd better release Springett or the cuffs will break his wrist. Also he could be useful to us up here."

She had done that, and Springett had stepped on deck and straight into a foaming wave that washed over the bow and took him with it. She'd been sad and appalled. Wyatt had registered no emotion at all and, once he'd found calmer waters in Westernport Bay, had gone below and laced her coffee with Mogadon.

"Did you hear me, Sergeant Redding? Your suspension will take effect from Friday. In the meantime I want you available for further questioning."

Liz blinked out of her daze. "Yes, sir."

They all left the room. Outside, in the corridor, cleaners had been splashing disinfectant around. Shoe-black streaked the floor and the bottoms of the walls. Liz's head felt heavy, heavy. Before she could stop herself, she veered toward Montgomery. Their shoulders touched. They sprang apart.

"Go home and rest, Sergeant."

Liz made him stop and face her, in this building that was never still, phones ringing, doors opening and closing. "But I stopped Springett, sir. I arrested him. A bent policeman, a senior officer. Surely that counts for something?"

Gosse was hovering behind them. He shoved forward. "Sergeant, if we had the jewels, if we had Wyatt, we might be inclined to go along with your story."

He shrugged. "As things stand now, you're history."

Chapter 7

Steer's jaw dropped. "Pentridge?"

"Yep."

"How come?"

"Because you're a piece of shit," the Correctional Services officer said.

They were waiting at a reception window in the new, privately operated remand center in Sunshine. Steer had been remanded on a charge of aggravated burglary, bail denied, and as he understood it you got sent to one of the remand centers pending trial, so why was the system stuffing him around today, turning him away, sending him to Pentridge prison?

"You're joking, right?"

Someone came through from an inner room with a form on a clipboard. The Correctional Services officer signed it and turned to escort Steer out to the police van again. Steer said, "I mean, how come? Tell me you're joking. I'm on remand, mate. I haven't been to trial yet."

The officer said wearily, "Can it, okay? The paperwork says 'Anthony Steer, remanded to Pentridge.'"

"But it's a fucking gaol, mate. It's full of blokes that'd slit your throat because they only got one egg for breakfast."

"You've done time before. You can handle it."

Steer could handle it. The problem was, Denise and Chaffey were lining someone up to spring him out of remand. Escaping from Pentridge was a whole other ballgame. He'd have to get Chaffey to do some fancy footwork with Correctional Services, slip someone a few bucks to alter the paperwork.

They bundled Steer into the rear of the police van. Steel floor, walls and ceiling, tiny reinforced glass window, plenty of steel separating him from the driver and the driver's offsider. He was the only prisoner. He heard the bolt slide home on the door of the van. He heard the Correctional Services officer tell the driver, "Remand's full. They've got room for him in Pentridge."

"Doesn't make sense," the driver said. "You've got remanded guys in Pentridge and sentenced guys in remand. Doesn't make sense."

"Tell it to the Minister."

The van braked and spurted fitfully through the western suburbs of the city. At Pentridge, in Coburg, the world seemed to darken, all light and goodness swallowed up by the bluestone walls. They were waved through. Steer's escort parked the van against an inside wall and disappeared for an hour. Steer grew jumpy in his metal tomb. When the doors of the van were finally opened, he said, "Morning tea, right? Your boss know you boys bludge on the job?"

"Shut it, arsehole."

They took Steer in to be admitted. A prison officer said, "Name?"

The driver of the van checked a sheaf of papers in his fist. "Steer, first name Anthony."

"*Anthony*, wacky doo," the prison officer said, ticking something. "Right, he's ours now."

Steer watched his escort walk back across the industrial-grade carpet and out through the door to the van. He swung back to the prison officer. "Look, I shouldn't be here. I should be in remand."

"Every remand center in the city is full, pal. That's why you're being remanded here, in D Divison."

"That's better than H Division, right?"

Steer had spent gaol time in Long Bay, Beechworth, Ararat, and Yatala. But he knew all about Pentridge. H Division was high security. It held killers, gunmen, escapers, men with a history of violence toward the prison guards, let alone other prisoners. Some inmates were handcuffed whenever they left their cells, even to have a shower. Others were kept in separation for months at a time, with only two hours out of the cell each day.

"Marginally," the prison officer said. He handed Steer a stack of clothing. "Put these on."

The shirt was thin from repeated washing, the collar frayed. The trousers stopped at his ankles. Both knees had worn through at some stage and been mended with patches on the inside and a crosshatch of thick black cotton thread. The windcheater, once chocolate brown, barely came to his waist. The shoes needed reheeling.

Wearing these clothes would be like wearing the skin of every pathetic junkie and rock spider who had ever been incarcerated in Pentridge. "No fucking way, mate."

The officer stiffened. "Come again?"

"I mean, give us a set of new gear and I'll make it worth your while."

"Yeah? How much?"

"Fifty."

"Make it seventy-five and you've got yourself a deal."

"My lawyer will slip it to you tomorrow."

"If he doesn't," the officer said, "then you go back to wearing castoffs."

"For seventy-five," Steer countered, "you can chuck in a decent set of bedding."

Finally an officer escorted Steer out of the administration wing. One inmate whistled on the long walk to his cell. Others stopped to stare as he passed among them. They approached a door. An inmate who had been leaning on the wall, smoking, sprang forward and opened the door, making a big show of it, doing Steer a favor.

Steer knew what it was about. It was a test. If he said thanks, he'd be marked out as a soft target. Steer wasn't soft. He was hard and lithe and very fit. Tall, narrow through the hips but broad at the shoulder, with a flat stomach and big hands, the knuckles like pebbles under the skin. There was scar tissue on his face but it was a grinning, clever, likeable face with bright killer's eyes and bad teeth. He stared at the man, cold and unnerving, and saw him drop his gaze and step back.

The guard watched it happen. "Piss off, Bence."

"Right you are, Mr. Loney, sir."

They were in a corridor of simple cells and Steer could see two bunks in each. The cells were poorly lit, about three cubic meters, the walls exuding bitter cold and dampness. Two men were hovering at the open door to the cell at the end of the corridor. "New bloke," they said.

Steer gave them the stare. Like Bence, they fell back. So far so good.

The guard said, "This is your cell, Steer. The charmer on the bottom bunk there is Monger. You'll show Steer here the ropes, won't you, Monger?"

"Sure, Mr. Loney," Monger said.

The guard left them to it. One of the men at the door wandered away. The other, leaning against the jamb, shook a cigarette from the packet in his top pocket. "Welcome to D Division, matey. Smoke?"

Steer said, "No thanks." It might have been a genuine offer, it might also have been a test.

"Suit yourself," the man said, wandering off.

Steer turned to Monger. Monger was young, nervy looking. "Mate, you're in my bed."

Monger sat up in the bunk. "What?"

"Yours is the top bunk."

Monger opened and closed his mouth. Finally he nodded, stripped the bedding from his bunk, and climbed onto the top bunk, far from the floor and the crapper, up where the farts gathered—all of which told Steer that this was Monger's first time.

Steer made himself comfortable. At lunchtime he saw Monger bend even further. He was at a scuffed table behind Monger, and watched as Bence and another man sat on either side of Monger and went to work.

First, Bence leaned forward. He fingered Monger's watch strap. "Nice."

Steer saw Monger jerk back his arm.

"Steady on," Bence said. "Just looking."

Monger nodded warily.

"Wouldn't have any smokes, would you?" the other man said. "I'm fresh out."

Monger had been given his prison issue. He got them out but before he could offer one Bence grabbed the entire packet and slipped it into his top pocket.

"Hey, come on," Monger said.

"Mate, you owe me."

"Owe you? How come?"

The other man was looking at Monger's food. He reached across, helped himself to the pudding and started to spoon it into his mouth. "Hungry," he explained, catching Monger's eye.

Monger said, "I suppose I owe you as well?"

Both men ignored him. Bence peered around him to the other man. "What duties they got you on this arvo?"

"Cleaning the shithouse."

"Get Monger to help you."

Monger protested. "I asked for the library."

"I bet you did, but that's too good for a little shit like you. I'd hate for you to get bored in here. I mean," Bence went on, "do a bloke a favor, you expect one in return, right?"

"Absolutely," the other man said.

Much later, back in the cell, Steer found Monger curled on the floor at the foot of the bunks, tired and dirty, his face streaked and miserable. "Come on, don't chuck in the towel."

Monger let himself be helped to his feet. Steer brushed him down, told him to change his clothes. "Mate," he said, "I could see it happening a mile off. I watched it all."

"So why didn't you give us a fucking hand?" Monger said, fighting down his self-disgust, his jitters.

"A few basic survival rules," Steer said, "all right? One, from now on, especially out in the yard, you're a marked man. The heavy boys like Bence will give you a hard time, stand in your way, shove you around, stuff like that. If you try and avoid them, go around them, you might as well curl up in a ball and die. You'd be theirs for good. Bum buddy in the shower. What you have to do is take them on. If you make eye contact, don't back down. Give them the old thousand yard stare. They'll beat the crap out of you, but at least you'll earn yourself some respect."

He broke off to look Monger up and down. "Jesus, you got it wrong from the start, didn't you?" He flicked his fingers at Monger's worn shirt, his patched trousers. "Look at this gear they gave you. You shouldn't have accepted it. Same goes for smokes. In here you only accept the offer of something if it comes from a close mate, not some bloke you don't know. Marks you out as weak, accept anything, unable to stand up for yourself. Plus, you'd then owe the guy something in return. That's what that was all about with Bence this afternoon."

"So why are you helping me?"

Steer said, "Don't like to see a young bloke stuffed around."

"I'm not a poofter. I tell you that right now."

"Didn't say you were. I'm not either. But we got to pass the time away, right? Might as well give you a few pointers."

In fact, Steer liked to lecture young crims. It was a side of him that could be irritating, but he couldn't help himself. He liked to point out where they'd gone wrong. Partly he got a kick out of it, partly he was reminding himself of where he'd stuffed up in the past, and partly it earned him respect—if he didn't push it.

The next day they called to say he had a visitor. He was escorted to a room that smelt of hopelessness. Denise was waiting for him. She gave him a watery smile, and a kind of sadness settled in Steer.

The visitors' room was like a cheap café, a place of scraping chairs, shouted conversations, coughing smokers, and general defeat. Poverty, that was the word, poverty. This was a world of poor men and their poor families. Their clothes were cheap, their haircuts and shoes, their ambitions. Every man in the room had showered and shaved that morning, but most had used soap in place of shampoo, and wore bad shaves from blunt electric razors, and generally looked unwashed and unkempt. It was no place to be meeting your bird.

Steer shook off the sadness. He became vigorous and sharp. "Great to see you, sweetheart."

"Great to see you, too."

"Chaffey's got to get me into remand."

Denise touched the back of his hand. "I saw him this morning. He's working on it."

Steer gave her a loaded look. "Any other news?"

"He rang before I left. He's confident."

Steer snarled. "Confident? What does he think I pay him for? I want results."

Chapter 8

Vallance and Allie said the Windsor Hotel, asked if he could pick them up and give them a lift to their place in Westernport. Maybe they didn't own a car, maybe they didn't drive—whatever, when Raymond left Chaffey he walked back to his apartment so that he could change and collect the keys to his XJ6, then he drove to the Windsor, parked outside and called up to their room on the courtesy phone.

"On our way," Vallance said.

Raymond went back to the car and waited. There was still a lot of cop activity in the center mile of the city. The Windsor. Clearly Vallance and Allie weren't short of a bob or two—unless it was all for show.

As he waited, he let himself think about Chaffey's proposal. A hundred grand for lifting a collection of paintings was better money at a lower risk factor than robbing a bank, so it was worth thinking about—if he were able to find himself a good partner.

According to Chaffey, art theft was the world's most lucrative crime after drug dealing. Stolen paintings found their way into private collections, were used as a stake in buying and selling arms and drugs, sold to crooked gallery owners and dealers for a third of their retail value, or sold back to insurance companies or owners for the reward money. Police in Australia had only a twenty percent clear-up rate. They were forced to sift through computerized records that listed stolen chainsaws and laptop computers alongside Picassos and Renoirs. Security was costly for most gallery owners and most private collectors kept inadequate records.

As Chaffey put it, there was only a 48-hour window of opportunity for lifting the paintings. The building where they were housed was undergoing a renovation, and for 48 hours—a Saturday and a Sunday—the power would be switched off and the paintings locked away in a storeroom. No cameras, no alarms, for 48 hours. Just a few locked doors and a nightwatchman every now and then through the night.

Twenty minutes later, Allie and Vallance appeared with their cases. They wore jeans and polo shirts, designer quality. Raymond found both of them hard to figure out. The jeans hung loosely on Vallance's bony hips and he looked all wrong, somehow too old for the picture he was presenting to the world. Allie didn't, so what was she doing with him? Raymond wanted to peel her open like a piece of fruit.

Vallance got into the back seat. Allie slid into the passenger seat and her long thighs filled Raymond's imagination. Vallance leaned into the gap between the seats. "Now, this is a no-obligation trip, okay? You don't have to commit yourself. Spend the night at our summer place and we'll take a boat out in the morning, look at the wreck, then you think about it. But I'll ask you to keep this confidential. I think you understand."

"No drama," Raymond said.

He fired up the Jaguar and slid into traffic. Neither Allie nor

Vallance said anything about the car, as though they were born to luxury.

"You were talking about some old newspaper clipping," Raymond prompted, watching Vallance in the rearview mirror.

Satisfaction and passion mingled on the man's narrow face. "Got it right here," he said, opening a document wallet. "You know, it can be like detective work, hunting down old wrecks. You accumulate apparently random fragments of information and look for the patterns and answers. Often what you get are false leads; you find yourself exercising your mind about the wrong problem."

He paused, staring into space. Raymond groaned inwardly. He was about to learn more than he needed to know, but the world was full of Vallances, full of tidy, narrow, pointless passions.

"In eighteen twenty-seven," Vallance said, "a barque called the *Eliza Dean* was reported missing between Sydney and Hobart. She'd sailed with a handful of passengers, plus provisions, plus fifty thousand quid's worth of gold, silver, and copper coinage. Can you imagine what that would be worth today?"

Raymond allowed himself to look awed. He sensed Allie next to him, her secret, almost conniving smile.

"Gold and silver coins, mostly. Also bank notes, checks and the royal mail. Most of the coins were bound for the garrison stationed in Hobart Town. The officers and soldiers hadn't been paid for some time."

Raymond steered with one hand, fished out his Spanish dollar with the other. "You think this came from the *Eliza Dean*?"

"I'm sure of it. The date is right, all the other wrecks and missing ships around that period have been accounted for, and none was carrying currency. You want to know how I worked it out?"

"Sure."

"At first I thought Bass Strait pirates. What they'd do was

build bonfires on the shores of King Island during fogs and lure ships ashore. They'd loot anything they could use—cutlasses, pistols, knives, clothing, food, tools—and store it all on Robbins Island. One story I heard, a woman was washed ashore wearing diamond rings. What did they do? They chopped off her fingers to get the rings. They'd fight amongst themselves. They'd drink, trade women, disappear without trace."

"Charming," Raymond said.

Allie turned to him, smiling her smile. "Of course," she said, "we've come a long way since then in relations between men and women."

Raymond thought: *Maybe he hits her, the bastard.* He coughed, glanced into the rearview mirror. "You thought pirates got the *Eliza Dean?*"

"I did," Vallance said. "Then I thought, no, why would she be sailing that far west? The Cornwall Group, islands about seventy k's southeast of Wilsons Promontory seemed like a better bet. A score of vessels have come to grief there. Thick sea fogs, howling gales, no lighthouse until the eighteen forties."

"So we'll be diving in howling gales and thick fogs?" Raymond asked.

"Nope. Where I found the coins we can anchor in sheltered waters, safely spend weeks exploring the reefs there if we wanted to. Want to know how come I focused on the Cornwall Group and not Flinders Island or the east coast of Tassie?"

"Sure." Raymond wound the big car past the Melbourne Cricket Ground. The big lights loomed coldly like spy cameras.

"Okay, listen to this. *Hobart Town Courier*, eighteen twenty-seven. It's what I mean by piecing clues together."

Vallance waved a photocopy between the seats, then settled back to read aloud. "Blah, blah, blah . . . *Captain Whitby, master of the Government cutter,* Swordfish, *was dispatched to make a search among the Bass Strait Islands for tidings or wreckage of the missing brig,* Mary May. *Captain Whitby reported on his return that considerable wreckage from the* Mary May *had been discovered on Clarke and Preservation Islands, but no trace of her passengers or crew.*

"Nevertheless a curious but related fact has emerged as a result of Captain Whitby's search. Whilst at anchor under the Cornwall Group during the term of a powerful gale, Captain Whitby had occasion to take the ship's vessel to the nearest shore, where he came upon a sealer living with two native women. The sealer, Sydney Dan by name, was unable or unwilling to provide a satisfactory account for the presence in his hut of certain items, namely a sea chest, a snuff box, numerous pistols, and a major's uniform. Furthermore, part of a deckhouse had been converted for use as a pigsty roof. Having ascertained that none of these items belonged to the Mary May, *Captain Whitby questioned the man more closely. His answers appeared to be most evasive, and Whitby returned to the* Swordfish *with his curiosity and suspicion considerably aroused.*

"Next morning Captain Whitby returned to the island and, taking the native women aside for questioning, discovered a cooked leg of mutton, a ham, and a cushion. Pursuing his inquiries farther afield, among sealers, fishermen and sailors from diverse parts of the Bass Strait Islands, Captain Whitby learned that numerous sealers had recently arrived in Launceston bearing checks, gold coins, and bank notes for which they could not give a clear accounting. One man possessed a ship's studding sail boom, with the sails still attached.

"The mystery has since deepened. The Courier *has it on good authority that Captain Gibb, Port Officer at Hobart Town, last month received anonymously in the post the register and other papers from the* Eliza Dean, *a barque missing between Sydney Town and Hobart Town this past half year. Further to this, letters which could only have been carried by the* Eliza Dean *recently arrived at their destinations in Hobart Town, postmarked Launceston.*

"Grave concern is held for the Eliza Dean, *if indeed she was lost upon*

*the reefs surrounding the Cornwall Group. There is a dereliction of duty
on the part of the Government if immediate steps are not taken to unravel
the mystery that enshrouds the fate of the thirty individuals on board. It
is a matter of importance to know whether they were drowned or murdered,
and whether they landed alive or if the bodies were plundered after being
washed ashore."*

Raymond frowned. "Yeah, yeah, yeah, but how do we know
the treasure is still on the wreck? It sounds as if she was looted
before she broke up. The coins you found could have been a
handful that got left behind."

He saw Vallance smile complacently. "Trust me, I know. I've
already made several passes with a metal detector and accounted
for all of the ferrous metals. The rest is solid gold and silver."

Gold. The word lodged in Raymond's head. He found himself
braking hard to avoid ramming the rear of a taxi on the approach
to the southeastern freeway at Hoddle Street.

As the endless suburbs slipped past their windows, Raymond
asked questions. They were as hard and knowing as he could make
them. He wasn't an easy catch. He didn't want them to *think* he was.

"You're looking for investors, fifty grand each. What does my
fifty grand buy me?"

"A sixth share in the treasure. Me, Allie, you, and three
others. Equal sixths."

"I don't mean that. I mean, what kind of expedition are we
mounting here?"

He sensed Allie shift in her seat. She was looking at him, her
knees swivelled toward him. Raymond had read about that in a
book on body language. If they cross one leg over the other or face
away from you, they were unconsciously saying they didn't want
to screw you. Allie wasn't saying that. She was saying she wanted
him, clear as day. Raymond almost didn't hear Vallance say:

"We need a ship we can live on in comfort for a few days.

Something with a winch and a fair-sized deck and hold area. We'll need different types of metal detectors, sonar gear, underwater video, an airlift, underwater scooters, maybe even a prop wash."

Those were just words to Raymond. He was more interested in concealment. "I get the impression you don't want anyone knowing about this expedition, so how do you propose to outfit it and spend a few days searching without being noticed?"

"You're right," Vallance said smoothly. "Why should we arouse the curiosity of others? I intend to hire a good boat in one port, the gear in a range of other ports around Victoria and Tasmania."

"Do we need all that gear?"

"That coin you've got there is one of a handful I found on a quick dive. The rest have been buried by the action of the tides. They'll need some getting at. It's been a hundred and seventy years, after all."

"I've scuba dived, but that's all," Raymond said.

"That's good enough for tomorrow's dive. It's just exploratory. I guarantee you won't be disappointed. When the time comes to mount a salvage dive, I'll do the diving. I've got hours of experience."

"How long?"

"The salvage itself?"

Raymond nodded.

"Several days, maybe a couple of weeks. We have to locate the wreck first—"

"I thought you already had."

"What I found were loose coins shaken free by the tides. The actual wreck, where the majority of the treasure is, could be some distance away after all this time. It might have broken up and be scattered over several hundred meters. So we locate the wreck, then make a plot chart of the overall site, then we start excavating, marking all our finds on the chart. That'll give us a better picture of the spread pattern."

They were off the freeway now, heading south on Dandenong–Hastings Road, past waterlogged farmland. Raymond looked at his watch. Almost time for lunch.

"When do we go out?"

"First thing in the morning," Allie said, her soft growl almost in his ear as she shifted to get comfortable.

Raymond liked her voice. "So I stay the night at your summer place."

"Be it ever so humble," Vallance said.

"Do you have your own boat?"

"We have a friend who runs a charter operation. He'll take us out in the morning."

"Good old Quincy," Vallance said.

"Good old Quincy," Allie agreed.

Raymond frowned. "How many people are in on this?"

Allie's cool fingers touched his wrist. "It's all right. Quincy's not involved. So far we've lined up three of the four investors."

Raymond's draw dropped. "*Three* of the four? Already? Who are they?"

Vallance seemed to close down. "You'll understand that they don't want their identities revealed. These are professional men. They've paid their fifty thousand."

"What if I say no?"

"Then no hard feelings. We'll approach one of our other contacts. It's just that you appeal to us. These are old geezers we're talking about. To them it's just another investment. They've got no soul, no romance in their veins. Someone like you, likes to hear the stories, willing to come out and dive with us, willing to have an open mind and not tie us up with lawyers and accountants—that's what we want for our fourth investor."

Raymond was silent. He felt a gut-clench of anxiety, a feeling that he might miss out entirely if he didn't act soon.

They drove over the railway tracks on the outskirts of Hastings, Vallance directing Raymond to a run-down flat in a block of four, several streets back from the waterfront. Again, Raymond couldn't work them out. It was an ugly little flat. They unpacked and drove to a café at the marina. One hour passed. Two. They made small talk. Raymond guessed that Allie and Vallance were maintaining a delicate silence around the topic of his investing with them, and so didn't want to pressure or confuse him. After a while they left him to think, saying they were going to make arrangements with their charter-captain friend, Quincy.

Raymond ordered another coffee and stretched his legs. Gulls wheeled above the café tables. Sail rigging pinged on the dry-docked yachts. He blinked, taking in the man who was staring moodily at the chalked menu.

"Uncle Wyatt?" he said, his old name for his father's brother.

Chapter 9

It had been a while since Wyatt had been called that. He knew of only one person in the world who'd called him that, but Wyatt distrusted coincidence and didn't turn around, not until he'd sought out the voice in the mirror behind the cash register. Still Wyatt didn't respond. He ran a checklist of his senses. They were a barometer of the town, the marina, the café itself. The place *seemed* all right: scratchy muzak, idle yachting types, tourists, the clank of café cutlery. Finally he said, "Ray?" and turned to his nephew.

Raymond unfolded from a plastic chair and grinned awkwardly. "Been a long time."

Wyatt was shocked. It was as if his brother stood there, languid, graceful, knockabout, wearing a likeable grin. But in the case of Wyatt's brother there had always been sour grievances under the grin. A lot of people, like Ray's mother, hadn't seen that until it was too late.

Wyatt stepped forward and shook the boy's hand. "Ray."

Boy—hardly a boy. If this were a normal occasion and Wyatt a normal man he might have said something like, "You've certainly shot up," or "The last time I saw you you were knee high to a grasshopper," but Wyatt had nothing mindless to say.

Instead, he looked at his grown-up nephew and asked, aware of the suspicion in his voice: "What brings you here?"

Raymond sensed it. "Don't worry, I'm not tailing you if that's what you think. I'm here with some friends." He searched for the term he wanted. "Fishing trip. You? On holiday?"

It occurred to Wyatt that he hadn't had a holiday in his life, just long stretches of idle, recuperative time between heists, periods spent resting his body but not his head. There was always the next job to plan, for when the money ran out. He clapped a hand shyly on his nephew's shoulder. "Good to see you," he said.

Raymond seemed to fill with pleasure. "Sit," he said, signalling to the waitress. "Beer? Something stronger?"

Wyatt shook his head. "Not for me."

At once Raymond went still. "You're not working on something?" He looked around the marina, as though banks and payroll vans had materialized there.

Wyatt allowed himself to smile. He watched carefully as Raymond turned to signal the waitress again. The last time Wyatt had seen the boy was fifteen years ago, when they'd put his father in the ground—Wyatt's brother, a man weak and vicious enough to blacken the eyes and crack the ribs of his wife and kid whenever the world let him down. In the end the world had disappointed him all the way to the morgue. Raymond had been ten at the time, fine-boned and quick like his mother, laughter always close to the surface. He'd had a black eye at the funeral, Wyatt recalled, and it was clear how he'd gotten it. He'd shown no emotion when the family tossed dirt into the yawning grave, only satisfaction. The official story was that Wyatt's brother had pitched headfirst from a flight of steps, onto a concrete floor. He'd been drinking heavily. Wyatt had gone with the accident story—until he saw Raymond at the graveside. Then he'd known it wasn't an accident, or mostly not.

"More coffee here," Raymond told the waitress.

Wyatt had known that his brother was no good. He'd tried to help, giving the family money, giving his own brother hard warnings to play it straight with his wife and son. It hadn't been enough, and later, after the funeral, they lost touch with one another. It seemed to be the best thing to do. Raymond had been getting too interested in the stories that surrounded Wyatt, making them add up to something more than the truth, until he'd asked, at the wake: "Can I live with you, Uncle Wyatt?"

"What have you been doing?" Wyatt said now.

"This and that." Then, slyly, "Not checking up on me, are you?"

Wyatt said nothing. He searched deep behind the open face. If Raymond was a user, his body would betray him. The boy's eyes were clear. No twitches. If Raymond were somehow wrong inside, like the man who'd fathered him, that might reveal itself as well. Wyatt needed to know.

The waitress came with their coffees. For a moment, Wyatt wondered if he'd seen something in Raymond, but now it was gone. He blinked, and saw Raymond sitting across from him, cool, very collected.

For the next thirty minutes, they talked, Wyatt keeping the conversation away from himself, away from questions about the past, always shifting the focus back onto Raymond. He had no use for small talk and an abhorrence of the world knowing anything about him. If he had to be the focus, he stuck to an abbreviation of the present. But Raymond was equally withholding. To cover it, he sometimes made absurd wagers.

"Bet you five the woman drives," he said, nodding at an elderly couple crossing the car park to their car.

Finally he said, "So, Uncle Wyatt, let's cut the crap. What are you doing here?"

"Going home."

"Home? No point asking where that is?"

Wyatt didn't reply.

As if to say, "I'm a better man than you are," Raymond fished out a pen and scribbled on the back of a coaster. "This here's my address and phone number. Look me up next time you're passing through Melbourne."

Wyatt nodded.

"Look, no more bullshit," Raymond said. Color and embarrassment showed on his face. "Those country banks? The bush bandit? That's me."

Wyatt waited for it to sink in. He felt faintly shocked. After a moment, he said flatly, "The bush bandit."

He supposed that it could be true. Raymond wasn't boasting, just stating who he was now. Wyatt had no wish to offer advice or warnings to his nephew, and there was nothing at risk for himself, so he decided to leave it at that.

"Never been caught, never even been a suspect. I work alone. If I pick up something I can't offload, there's a guy who'll do it for me."

"Maybe I know him."

"Chaffey. Lawyer in the city."

Wyatt shook his head. He was out of touch.

"Chaffey knows *you*," Raymond said. "I mean," he said hastily, catching the stiffening of Wyatt's face, "he knows you're my uncle, that's all, knows all the stories about you, knows we don't have anything to do with each other. He hasn't sent me to track you down, if that's what you're thinking."

"Good."

"Although," Raymond said, "he did mention a job to me."

Wyatt waited. He could see now that Raymond had been working up to this. "I see."

"I more or less turned it down," Raymond said. "It's an art collection, outside my field, plus I'd need a partner and I don't know anyone I trust enough to work with."

Wyatt felt a stir of interest, almost an itch. "What sort of art collection?"

Raymond outlined the job swiftly. "Worth a hundred grand," he concluded. "Chaffey's got a buyer already lined up."

Wyatt kept stony-faced. A hundred thousand dollars, split two ways.

"Think about it, Uncle Wyatt. This is right up your alley. I wouldn't know a print from a poster."

Wyatt felt his nerve endings stir. He looked around the marina, looking for the trap. "You sure you're not following me?"

Raymond's face darkened. "Fuck you. For fifteen years I haven't known where you were. How could I follow you? Pure coincidence."

"Okay, okay."

"So, you interested?"

"I'll let you know."

Gloomily Raymond began to shred a paper napkin. "Don't suppose you need the money. You must have stashed a fair bit away over the years."

Wyatt couldn't tell his nephew about the big jobs that had gone wrong, the stuff he'd left behind, the pissy jobs in the past couple of years. A kind of sadness settled in him. If he'd stepped in all that time ago, he could have saved Raymond from a world in which the only men he had to model himself upon were brutes like his father and holdup men like his uncle. Raymond had grown up too quickly and seen too much too soon. Wyatt tried to name the source of his sadness. It was composed of many things, among them guilt, sadness for his brother's short, failed life, a renewed sense of responsibility for Raymond.

All of these things, but mostly his memory of that last meeting, when Raymond was ten and had seen his father into the ground and had turned to Wyatt and asked, "Can I live with you, Uncle Wyatt?"

"Raymond, my boy, there you are."

Wyatt felt his interest wane and his wariness return. A man and a woman, the man a skinny character in his fifties, the woman a lithe, pouting fluffball in her twenties.

"Um, meet my fishing mates," Raymond said.

He named the man as Brian Vallance, the woman as Allie Roden, and told them that Wyatt was an old family friend. "Known Macka since I was a kid," he said.

Wyatt shook the woman's hand briefly, then the man's. The man held on, slowly squeezing, testing Wyatt.

A waste of time. Wyatt shook his head irritably and withdrew his hand. He didn't like the man or the woman, and watched them when they were all seated. Vallance wore the pout of a man convinced that he'd never exercised choice, that his failures were none of his doing but the result of the raw deals that life had thrown up for him—the bad luck, accidents and treachery of others. He wore costly jeans and Wyatt saw him tug the fabric away from his knees carefully and smooth it under his thighs whenever he shifted in his seat. The woman was playing some kind of game. She was with Vallance, but giving Raymond soulful looks. And once, when the other two men were not looking, Wyatt found her looking long and hard at him.

"You a fisherman, Macka?" she asked, a slow heat in her face and her voice.

Wyatt shook his head. He climbed to his feet. "Not me." She was slippery. He had to get away. Unaccountably, then, he thought of Liz Redding.

Chapter 10

She was under orders from Gosse not to leave the building before five. He'd call her in every couple of hours for another bout of questioning, sometimes with Montgomery in attendance, sometimes with the faceless men from the Internal Investigations branch. It was always the same thing: they wanted times, dates, places, names, and they wanted her to account for her motives in going to Vanuatu and coming back with a known crook.

Liz chafed through the day. At one point a friend came by and whispered, "Mate, they're searching your locker."

Mate, Liz thought. Man or woman, you're everyone's mate in the police. It was a life built for mates, all differences levelled out, including gender. But one false step and they soon reminded you how different you were.

She found Gosse there, supervising. "Go back to your desk, Sergeant."

"You have no right—"

"I have every right."

"You think I've got the jewels hidden in my tracksuit pants? Think I've got a valentine from Wyatt hidden in my tampon box?"

Gosse turned, snarling, "Nothing about you would surprise me. Back to your desk, Sergeant."

Liz went back. She felt the beginnings of a shift in the way she viewed the world. She wanted to find Wyatt but realized that she no longer wanted to find him on behalf of the Victoria Police. She hunted the files for an address. When Wyatt had first come to her attention he'd been trying to offload stolen goods. Liz had posed as a fence, and the man who'd led Wyatt to her was Jardine, a burnt-out thief and friend of Wyatt's. Jardine had since died, but his sister Nettie might know something.

At five o'clock Liz drove to a flat, depressed corner of Coburg, where small weatherboard and brick-veneer houses breathed into one another's mouths and old women and men broke their hips on the root-buckled footpaths. The paint was flaking on Nettie Jardine's house. One corner needed restumping and the external boards and frames harbored a deep, rotting dampness. It would be there even in midsummer, like an exhalation of hopelessness.

Nettie opened the sticking main door to Liz but not the screen door. She wore the cares of the world in her thin frame, her limp, pale hair, her narrow mouth. But a spark of something animated her sorrowing face when she saw Liz. "You again."

"Hello, Nettie."

"That's the shot, first names. What do I get to call you, your majesty?"

"I don't mind if you call me Liz."

Nettie Jardine sniffed. "Thought I'd finished with you lot."

"Just a couple of questions. Do you think I could—"

"Right here will do," Nettie said, folding her arms firmly behind the screen door.

"Right. About your brother—"

"He's dead."

"I know. I'm sorry."

"Sorry's not going to bring him back."

"Nettie, we're more interested in a man your brother was involved with. Wyatt."

"That bastard."

Liz said mildly, "I understand he was your brother's friend. Didn't he help out with rent, bills, living costs?"

"Guilt money."

"Your brother blueprinted burglaries for him, Nettie. He wasn't forced into it."

Nettie was stubborn. "Wyatt had influence over Frank."

Liz doubted that. She said, "What I need to know is, how did Frank get in touch with Wyatt? When Frank put a burglary or a robbery together, how did he pass on the photographs, the floor plans, the briefing notes?"

"Mail drop."

"You mean a holding address?"

"Call it what you want. He's paranoid. Doesn't like you to know where he lives."

Liz nodded. She had an impression of the unreality of her life. Wyatt's life, a secretive, complicated parallel life, seemed suddenly clearer and more appealing to her than her own. "So you've never seen his place."

Nettie shrugged. "Why would I?"

"Know anyone who has? His family, maybe?"

"Far as I know, there's only a nephew."

Liz sharpened at that. "Nephew?"

"Raymond Wyatt. Flash bugger."

"Where would I find him?"

Nettie laughed. "Try the bloody phone book."

Fair enough, Liz thought. "This mail drop. Where was it?"

"Hobart," Nettie muttered.

Hobart. The mail drop was probably inoperative now, given Wyatt's caution, but a man can't live in total isolation. He has wants and needs that bring him into contact with the wider world. He has dealings with dentists, doctors, real estate agents, local shopkeepers. Hobart was a small place. She could go down there, flash his photo around. It wasn't much of a likeness. It was a blurred, long-distance surveillance shot. Wyatt, eternally watchful, had never let himself be photographed clearly. Liz made a few impressionistic notes in her mind—tall, slender, graceful on his feet, big hands, rarely smiles, thin face, sharp lines with a dark cast to the skin.

"Where in Hobart?"

There was no humor in Nettie's smile. "Couldn't say, really. All I know is, you're too far away and too late."

"Nettie," Liz said warningly, "what's going on?"

"You wait and see. All I'm saying is, no one hurts the Jardines and gets away with it."

Chapter 11

On the outskirts of Hastings the cab driver caught Wyatt's eye in the rearview mirror. "You got a yacht down here?"

He wants to discuss sailing with me, Wyatt thought. To forestall that, he said, "Just been visiting for a few days."

"Like it?"

"Sure."

"People think this is a bit of a backwater, but we have our share of drama."

"Yes," Wyatt said.

"That kiddie abducted on the other side of the Peninsula, that killer up in Frankston. You'll even see in the marina a boat the police impounded. Something to do with smuggling from Vanuatu, one of them places."

Wyatt glanced out of the window. The taxi was passing swampy flatland. Beyond it was the refinery. A big tanker was in dock.

He let the driver talk on. Once inside the terminal at Tyabb aerodrome, he stood at the glass, gazing across the airstrip. Suddenly a shadow washed over the field, cutting off the sun briefly, and a harsh motor swamped the ordinary human sounds behind him. Wyatt looked up. A plane was barrelling in, hard and fast. It was squat-looking with a high cockpit, and it wore US Navy markings. It dated from the Second World War and Wyatt hadn't seen it for a while. He'd forgotten it. It used to roll and flip in the sky above his house behind Shoreham. He watched it sideslip against the crosswind and touch down, skipping a little before it settled into a fast run toward the hangars. It dwarfed the Cessnas and Pipers.

At four o'clock Wyatt and six other passengers boarded a twin-prop, ten-seater commuter plane. During the ascent, he watched the topography clarify into a school at a crossroads, a trucking firm, a motel, a sunflash in the distance from the refinery at Westernport, the wingless, snout-up DC3 in a corner of the airfield, then horse studs, wineries, small holdings, roads, and fences. The plane held a course southeast. This was a part of the world that Wyatt had crossed and recrossed a thousand times, on foot, in a car, in the air, often on the run from the law. He had staked life and a degree of contentment on it, using the little farmhouse somewhere below as his bolthole, slipping away from time to time to knock over a bank or a payroll van. That life had failed him in the end. But he knew the place, it had mapped itself in his brain and on his nerve endings.

Inverloch and the Victorian coast slipped by beneath him. King Island was ahead, and a separate flight to Hobart. The water looked choppy.

Wyatt allowed himself to think of Liz Redding again, and of their voyage from Vanuatu in the stolen yacht. For six days they had managed to forget who they were, but when the coastline of Australia appeared, Wyatt had found himself planning the next stage, escaping with the jewels. He hadn't known how to include Liz in his plans, so convinced himself that she wasn't a factor.

Liz had been more forthright. Running with him was out, she didn't want to lose him, which left an impossible alternative.

"Wyatt," she'd said, "let me bring you in."

Wyatt had shaken his head. Killings and millions of plundered dollars marked the years of his existence and the police of every state wanted a word with him.

"Out of the question," he said.

There was distress in her voice. "What about us?"

Wyatt had been unable to say anything. He'd stared at the sea, the rising chop on the surface of the water, the seabirds sideslipping above the white caps. The clouds had been scudding. There was plenty to be on guard against: the waves, iron shipping containers floating just beneath the surface, waiting to rip a hole in the hull.

And his feelings. Liz Redding was combative, bright, generous. She made him feel wanted, even loved. The word quivered there in his head, once he'd admitted it. Wyatt thought of her squirming naked energy, her wit and affection. But all that had become a complication. Old habits of preservation had kicked in.

"Wyatt? Are you deaf?" she'd demanded. "Have you thought about us at all?"

Into the silence that followed, Wyatt had muttered, "All the time."

He realized now, far above Bass Strait, that he was unused to conversation, unused to the slipperiness of a conversation like the one he'd had with Liz Redding. His disposition was built upon layers of secrecy and preservation, a lifetime's habit of believing that no one was dependable but himself. People found him resourceful and cautious, a man with a dark, rapid mind, who took nothing on trust and who could be trusted to place his safety before anything, but they always wanted more, a man with ordinary doubts and scruples and impulses. What they got was a man who shut himself down. They looked for the doors and windows in him but few ever found them. Liz Redding had come close, in those seven days. He liked that, but it scared him. He'd seen that a life with her might be possible. She was his way out, if he'd wanted that.

But he'd decided that he didn't want it. As the storm rose in intensity, he'd charted a course for Westernport Bay, a place he knew better than his own face in the mirror. It wasn't imperative that they dock in Westernport, but Wyatt hadn't told Liz Redding that. Old habits were kicking in and he was going to betray her.

He'd gone below, first to the packet of Mogadon in the medicine cabinet, then to the wall oven in the galley. It was set into the bulkhead and worked perfectly well as an oven, but it also slid out to reveal a small waterproof safe. Wyatt pocketed a roll of $100 notes, his .38 revolver and a distinctive necklace, and closed everything again, just as Liz Redding had called down to him, "Wyatt? Is everything all right?"

"Coming now."

He'd laced her coffee, then added a dash of Scotch, and carried it to her in the wheelhouse.

She let him take the wheel. She sipped her coffee. "Ah, hot, foul, and bracing."

Wyatt said nothing. He watched the heaving sea. It was not a companionable silence. All of the topics between them had been pushed as far as he was able to take them, and he was waiting, with sadness, for his final act of betrayal to take effect. In a mood of disconnection and apathy, they had sailed through the night.

Someone had once accused him of working from an emotionless base. He mused on that now, as the plane banked above the Bass

Strait Islands. He mused on it for half a minute, all it was worth, trying to picture the face he presented to the world. He knew it could be assertive, prohibitive, sometimes chilling, giving nothing away. Most people's faces were a barometer of their feelings. They bulged in all directions, chased by doubts, scruples, and conflicts. But it was not true that Wyatt was emotionless. He had room only for the essential ones, that's all, and he kept those to himself. Up until now, that hadn't been a problem.

The pilot's voice broke in upon his melancholy. They were descending.

Ten minutes later, Wyatt discovered that he would have to spend the night on the island.

The next morning, he was on the first flight out. When the plane touched down at Hobart Airport, Wyatt climbed into a taxi. There was always the risk that a cab driver would remember his face one day, but Wyatt had no intention of taking the airport bus to the city. Wyatt knew all about that bus. He'd been caught before. A good ten years older than airport buses anywhere else in the world, it would hum along the freeway and over the bridge and into the tight, one-way streets of Hobart, encouraging a sense of mission accomplished in its passengers. But then, unaccountably, it would begin to stop at the hotels, the motels, the casino way to hell and gone down Sandy Bay Road, dropping off passengers, before finally winding its way back to the downtown bus station, scarcely emptier than when it had set out, the majority obliged to wait for the chosen few. There was nothing democratic about that bus.

He paid off the taxi at the wharf opposite Salamanca Place, leaving him with a ten-minute walk to his apartment building. He'd never taken a cab all the way to the door in his life. He always concealed his final destination and covered his tracks. That was second nature to Wyatt. It was part of an automatic checklist that had kept him alive and out of gaol and mostly ahead since the day he was born.

The Mawson base supply ship was in dock. He idled for a while, watching crated food and equipment being winched aboard. The bow looked scraped, freshly wounded, as though the ship had ploughed through ice recently, leaving paint smears in its wake.

Wyatt turned to go. He stood for some time on the footpath, waiting for the traffic to clear, and came close to witnessing a death. A boy had ambled onto the road from the opposite footpath. He was about ten, undernourished, cheaply dressed, hair cropped short as though for fashion's sake but probably to control head lice. He was cramming a hamburger into his mouth, and the car that braked to avoid him, snout dipping with the raw, smoking bite of its tires, skewed violently and finally stopped, its front bumper gently knocking the boy's knees.

The world held its breath. One second. Two seconds. There was something wrong about the boy's reaction time. Then suddenly he spasmed with fright. One hand jerked involuntarily, scattering the hamburger. A kind of sulky defiance and embarrassment showed on his face. He sniggered. Wyatt knew exactly what it meant. The boy was saying, *"Missed me—but I wouldn't have minded if you'd run me down. Death—or food and a warm bed in hospital—would be better than the life I've got."* Wyatt felt that he knew the boy. His home was a place where you got smacked about the head and thrown across the room. Where a belt buckle drew your blood for no reason at all. It was a pathology Wyatt recognized.

Grief settled in him, dull and dark. Wyatt and his brother had had "uncles" when they were kids. One after the other. Those men hadn't stayed for long. They didn't want a couple of kids hanging around. They were bitter and afraid and their only solace was to witness fear in the two boys. Wyatt had made sure that they never saw it in him. His brother hadn't been so lucky.

Wyatt's brother had absorbed all of that bitterness and it had erupted when he had a son of his own, Raymond.

Wyatt glanced at his watch. Almost lunchtime. He decided to call in at his mail drop, a dingy barbershop on the other side of the downtown area of the little city. When he got there, the barber said, almost relishing it, "Nothing." Wyatt shrugged. He hadn't really been expecting mail or messages. He crossed back to the waterfront, climbed the Kelly Steps into Battery Point.

Wyatt lived on the ground floor of a squat, tan brick and white stucco block of flats overlooking the Derwent. He'd been there for a year, in this city where no one knew him, where no one cared that he came and went once a month or so, where no one connected his movements with a rifled office safe in Toorak, a hallway stripped of Streetons in Vaucluse, an empty jewellery box on the Gold Coast.

A man called Frank Jardine had put these jobs together for him, but Jardine was dead now, and Wyatt would have to go back to putting his own jobs together.

He turned left at the top of Kelly Street, crossed over and began to wind his way through the little streets, over the hump of Battery Point, toward the down slope on the other side. Wyatt was a good burglar, but only if he had a shopping list, and was acting on information supplied by someone like Jardine. His chief talent lay in hitting banks and payroll vans, hitting hard and fast with a team of experts. A wasted talent now, for all of the experts were gone. He still got "sweet" invitations from time to time, but knew that it was better to stay put than to make a mistake; better to reject the "sweet" money than risk his life or his freedom.

So, how "sweet" was Raymond's art heist?

Wyatt unpacked his bag and rested. That evening he made his way back to a bistro in Salamanca Place. He ordered wine and pasta, then coffee. In the old days there had been experts he could work with, men who could drive, bypass a security system, crack a safe, all without a shot being fired. Now there were only youngsters with jumpy eyes and muscle twitches, in need of a fix, their brains fried, as likely to shoot dead a cop or a nun as Wyatt himself if they felt mean enough, or paranoid enough, or heard enough voices telling them to do it. Or they talked too much before the job, boasting in the pub to their mates or their girlfriends, who then whispered it to the law.

He finished eating and walked back, misty rain blurring the street lights. As a potential partner, Raymond looked pretty good to Wyatt. It was in this frame of mind, assessing, reflective, that Wyatt let himself into his flat and into trouble.

Chapter 12

He should have taken a moment to clear his head before going in. He should have looked, waited, thought, had a backup plan ready, a way out.

For when he let the door close behind him, flicking on the light as he did so, all he got was the sound of the switch. The darkness was absolute.

Then an arm went around his neck and the twin barrels of a shotgun, apparently cut short with a hacksaw, tore the skin at the hinge of his jaw.

"Not a sound. Not a fucking *move*, mate."

Wyatt remained still, loose, and relaxed on his feet. His flat smelt ripe, lived in, an odor compounded of grievances and shot nerves and perspiration breaking through cheap talc; the odor of a man with the jitters.

"Bastard. Where you been?"

It was a rhetorical question. Wyatt said nothing.

"I'm going to search you."

"Okay."

At the moment the arm relaxed its hold on his neck and felt for and found the .38 in his waistband, Wyatt drove the heel of his shoe down the man's shinbone, then dropped like a rock from the man's grasp. The .38 fell to the carpet. Wyatt patted the carpet uselessly for a few seconds, then scooted away in the darkness. He sensed opposing inclinations in the man—the tearing pain, Wyatt at large and dangerous to him. "I'm gonna fucking kill you," the man said.

Wyatt heard a chair fall. He didn't search for another light switch, guessing that the power was off at the fuse box—the gunman's mistake, for now they were both blind. The man should simply have removed the bulb.

Wyatt listened, backed into a corner, straining his eyes to pick up stray light from the curtained windows. Unfortunately they faced the water; there were no street lights out there. But no one could get behind him, no one could see him, and he had a measure of control over the doors and windows if the man had friends with him.

"Bastard. I'll have you."

Wyatt was silent.

"Frank's dead because of you."

He's talking about Frank Jardine, Wyatt thought. *He must be the younger brother.* He risked a reply:

"Frank knew the score."

Frank Jardine had worked with Wyatt in the old days, hitting banks and security vans, before retiring to become a blueprinter, planning high-level burglaries for Wyatt from information supplied by croupiers, insurance clerks, taxi drivers, builders, tradesmen who installed alarms and safes, shop assistants. Then, while coming out of retirement to pull one more job with Wyatt, he'd been head-shot and suffered a series of strokes, and now was dead.

Wyatt had given money to the Jardines for his convalescence, but clearly that wasn't enough for the family.

Sometimes, late at night, it wasn't enough for Wyatt.

"He's dead because of you," the brother repeated now.

Wyatt had no intention of speaking again. Jardine's brother had made up his mind. Wyatt waited. After a period of cursing and carpet scraping, the man abruptly ceased moving, as though sharper instincts were finally kicking in. He was listening, just as Wyatt was listening, and he wasn't giving his position away.

Wyatt eased himself onto his back. It was pointless looking for the .38. He felt with his right hand until he found the old armchair that sat against the wall next to him. It wore a fussy beaded fringe around its base and Wyatt slipped his hand in and found the knife he'd taped to the lower frame.

The man heard him. A spurt of flame erupted from the shotgun and a wad of pellets tore through the armchair. Wyatt placed him. He uncoiled from the floor and plunged blade-first across the room.

The blade missed. Their shoulders collided but the blade slipped past, slicing the empty air.

They grappled. Jardine's brother was unused to close fighting. His instinct was to spring away from Wyatt and level the shotgun at him; Wyatt's was to hold him close, trapping the gun between them. Then, punctuated by the man's sobbing exertion and panic, Wyatt began to pull him onto the blade. He felt the initial resistance of cloth, skin, bone, then the blade was slipping between the bones of the ribcage. Jardine's brother uttered a soft "oh" of surprise. He released the shotgun. Wyatt felt him sway. A moment later he was lowering him to the carpet. There was a weakening pulse when he felt for it.

Wyatt found the fuse box and turned on the lights. He worked it out. The family knew about the mail drop. The brother had simply come to Hobart and staked it out, then followed Wyatt home. Now Wyatt had a body in his flat, pooling blood on his carpet and neighbors who might have heard the shotgun. It had all been unnecessary, but he supposed that he couldn't blame the Jardines. In Wyatt's game, there was always a simple accounting for people's actions. What mattered now was he had to find himself another bolthole.

Chapter 13

For Raymond it was a form of hell, sharing quarters with other people, getting up when they got up, sitting around a kitchen table with them, eating toast and eggs and drinking coffee, then waiting around through the long hours, waiting for them to do something, enduring their small talk. But he wasn't working solo now. He was working with other people and they had to be kept happy. It was necessary for the job, but he looked forward to that time after the job, when caring about the happiness of other people no longer meant anything and they could be jettisoned.

Or not quite. Maybe Vallance could be jettisoned. Allie was a different matter.

He watched them eat breakfast and it was hell. Allie and Vallance moved in a comfortable stale fog, jaws grinding, their faces puffy with sleep. Allie wore loose satin pyjamas that somehow, where they clung to her breasts and buttocks, suggested hot pliant skin. She was stunning. Vallance wasn't. He wore a towelling robe and looked creased and shambling and inert. Raymond tried to imagine the nature of their passion. He couldn't.

They had given Raymond the couch to sleep on. The sloping pitch of the base had threatened to stuff up his back for days, so at midnight he'd moved the cushions to the floor. He still slept badly. At 4:20 he'd awoken and seen, in the light of a digital clock, that Allie was crouched nearby, gravely watching him. He didn't think she'd been there long, for somewhere along the corridor the toilet stopped flushing. Raymond had breathed in audibly, ready to speak, but Allie had silenced him, kissing her fingers and laying them on his lips. He now wondered if he'd dreamt the whole thing. It had been erotic, sure, but somehow also tender, and he'd not had much of that in his life.

An hour later, fully showered and dressed, Vallance showed him a red vinyl Thomas Cook bag. "Told you I had a whole heap of coins," he said.

Raymond unzippered the bag, whistled at the sight of so many gold, silver, and bronze coins, plus small ingots, some of it melded together by a hard sediment. "Nice," he said.

"That it is," Vallance said. "Right, shall we go?"

Raymond drove the short distance back to the marina. Quincy was waiting for them, a grizzled character with an alcoholic's broken blood vessels in his face. He seemed incurious about Raymond, incurious about the purpose of the voyage. Raymond guessed he was paid to keep his trap shut.

Their passage out of Westernport Bay, toward the Cornwall Group of islands, induced in Raymond a sense of anticipation. He fingered the silver dollar in his pocket. It wasn't eagerness, hunger or greed. He'd be hard pushed to define any extreme of feelings. But he couldn't deny that all of his senses were alert, that the blood ticked in him inexorably, that he felt the prickling awareness of the hunter closing in. Hidden treasure. Buried treasure. His skin tingled. His mother had once said, "You're my treasure." Queer that he'd think of that now. He wasn't a man who had much time for looking back. The world was full of people crippled by regret for past actions and inactions. It got them nowhere. They didn't know how to forgive or accept themselves. Then again, the world was full of monsters who remained monsters exactly because they had no trouble forgiving themselves at all.

Raymond blinked, shaking off the trance, putting himself firmly in the here and now again, on the deck of a trawler, sailing in mild sunlight. Bass Strait was calm. Raymond was glad: his guts would have acted up on him otherwise. Five hours later, the islands appeared. Quincy steered toward a narrow boiling passage between reefs, heading for sheltered water beyond.

Raymond and Allie stood on the port side, Vallance on the starboard, reef-spotting while Quincy throttled back and picked a way through the gap. The boat pitched and jawed a little in the rougher water. It felt dangerous to Raymond, a gut-lurching sensation, but Vallance and Allie rode the twisting deck comfortably so he told himself it was nothing. The air felt cool and damp on his face, briny in his nostrils, and seabirds slipped in the air currents above him.

Then they were through, gliding across still water. Grey cliffs, a tiny pebbly beach set with large rounded boulders, a muttonbird rookery, a glimpse of treeless vivid grassland above the cliffs. Raymond tipped back his head and breathed the air. He felt alive, and then Allie was standing next to him. Her arms circled his waist briefly and her chin pressed him between the shoulderblades.

She released him. "Isn't this great?"

Her eyes were bright, keen, full of curiosity and simple happiness. It was infectious. Raymond felt an absurd need to reach out and dab at some poorly applied zinc cream on her nose. He allowed a brief glint of teeth. "Great."

Vallance dropped anchor and joined them. He was grinning, his thin face and wiry frame revelling in the moment. "Piece of cake."

"Lucky with the weather," Raymond said.

Vallance sobered. "I agree. I also have to say that time is a factor here. The wreck's in about twenty meters of water on the other side of the reef. In a few weeks' time what we're doing today won't be possible. Gale-force winds, heavy seas, you name it."

"In other words, if I'm going to put up the money for this it'll have to be soon."

Vallance coughed, looked embarrassed. "Well, yeah. That's why this'll be a quick visit. Take you out to the site, let you run the metal detector over the area, maybe dig up a few more coins, then head back to Westernport. Mate, we want you to see that this is a goer."

Raymond still had plenty of questions. He looked away from the island to the other islands in the group, small, barren humps in the sea. "Couple of boats anchored out there," he said.

"Fishermen."

"You haven't encountered other treasure seekers?"

"No."

"What about official visitors? I'm thinking of inspectors from that crowd you used to work for, the Maritime Heritage Unit."

"Nope."

Raymond stared at Vallance for a while. Gulls wheeled above the yacht. The air was fresh and sharp, bracing to breathe. Raymond couldn't let the air distract him, lead him away from his natural state, which was suspicion and scepticism. "Are there other wrecks here?"

"A score of them. They've all been charted."

"Excavated?"

"Those that matter. A big convict vessel went down in eighteen thirteen, for example. That had the historians interested. Most of the other ships were small intercolonial traders. Livestock, timber, stuff like that."

"So no one knows the *Eliza Dean* is here?"

"Not yet. But they will. Someone will stumble on her by accident sooner or later. That's why it's imperative we go in now."

"Why hasn't she been found?"

Vallance said impatiently, "You dive with me, you'll see why. When she hit the reef, the hull would've gone straight to the bottom, weighed down by ballast, crates of coins, other heavy stuff. It'll be under a few meters of sand by now. The rigging, masts, upper decking, anchors, general superstructure, well that would have been strewn over a wide area by tides and storms. We're talking about a hundred and seventy years, you know. From what I know about the tides here, the smaller stuff, including the few coins that worked loose or were grabbed by the crew, will have been scattered in a particular way."

He squatted on the deck, wet a finger, sketched two reefs and then a cone shape abutting one of them. Tapping the widest arc of the cone, he said, "Where I found the coins, plus a tin plate and a couple of buttons and spoons, approximates to here. What we have to do is crisscross back in this direction." He indicated the pointed end of the cone. "That's where the wreck itself will be."

"The mother lode."

"Exactly."

"You weren't so specific the first time you told me this."

"You weren't so interested."

Raymond looked out to sea, then back at the rapidly drying diagram. "You're saying it's between those two reefs?"

"Yes. The outer one is deeper. The *Eliza Dean* passed right over it, then struck the inner one. That's why no one's found her before."

"What if we do have an unexpected visitor, either now or when and if we mount an expedition? They'll know something is going on."

"I'm confident we won't have visitors, not this late in the season. But I can always dive at night or anchor some distance away and swim to the wreck from there. You're thinking telltale bubbles in the water? Simple. I'll use a rebreather."

"You're the expert," Raymond said.

"That he is," Allie agreed, embracing Vallance, resting her temple on his shoulder.

A kind of hatred flooded through Raymond. "One last question."

"Fire away. You're the man with the money."

"That's just it," Raymond said. "The world is full of fools with money to throw away. Why me? Why me and only three others? Why not a big consortium?"

From anyone else, these would have been first questions, but Raymond wanted Vallance with his hopes running high before he asked it. He wanted to see if Vallance would stumble or blanch or spin him a story.

What Vallance did under the wheeling sky, the wind in his sparse hair, was say, "I won't lie to you. It's a protected area. No diving allowed."

"Uh huh."

"That convict ship? It's pretty close to where I found the coins. It's fragile, excavation is going to take years. The government doesn't want looters, they don't want amateurs, they don't want anyone doing anything to disturb the wreck."

"So we'll be inviting arrest," Raymond said flatly.

Vallance nodded.

"That's why everything about this will have to be kept secret," Allie put in.

"With any luck," Vallance said, "the actual search will be quick. I did a preliminary survey the time I found the coins. Another survey today and tomorrow should help narrow the search area. Then when we come here with all the gear we simply vacuum up the sand, gather the coins, get away quick."

He paused. "Like I said, we need two hundred grand to get the show on the road. The return from your fifty grand will be in the millions. I'm not asking for fifty right away. If you can get twenty to me by the end of the week, that will secure your fifty grand stake in the syndicate."

After a while, Raymond nodded. "Okay."

Vallance clapped his hands together. "Time to get togged up, ladies and gentlemen."

Raymond went below, changed, reappeared on deck again. He found Allie and Vallance, in colorful wetsuits, checking the air tanks and regulators. They were both slight in build and in their vivid costumes reminded Raymond of glossy tropical frogs. Vallance handed him lead weights on a belt and a sheathed, chrome-plated knife. "Strap these on."

And then they slipped over the side and into the water. Vallance led the way, over the inner reef to deeper water. As they angled toward the bottom, a strange fear gripped Raymond, a sense of a fist closing over his lungs. He knew that his lungs were contracting. The water grew colder. He found himself sipping at the air. It seemed to be thick, weighty air, as though a liquid were pouring down into his lungs. He found that he was losing red from the color spectrum. A brand name stamped on the wristband of his wetsuit was being leached of redness. His heart pounded.

He looked about for Vallance and Allie. He couldn't see them. For several minutes he was suspended in murky water, then suddenly Allie was beside him, winking, pointing downward. Seeing her gave him back his nerve.

He gazed around after that, enjoying himself, and when he saw Vallance again the older man was standing on the bed of the sea, scooping his arms for balance, his flippers stirring the sand, and Raymond saw an old coin of the realm appear, then another, stamped with the king's name and a Latin script and a date more than 170 years before he was born.

Chapter 14

The coins—their tragic history, their weight and substance, their *goldness*—lodged in Raymond's head. He could feel want and fascination stirring inside him. In his mind's eye he saw the spill of gold on the seabed, and traced it back to the rotting hull and the laden chests. His share would make him a wealthy man. He hungered—for the hunt, the discovery, the division of the spoils, the addictive element of risk. He met these needs whenever he robbed a bank, but this time the take was buried treasure. Treasure. It was enough to make him dream.

But all he had in the world was a lifestyle and a promise. The lifestyle boiled down to clothes, a car, an apartment—but no money; and the promise boiled down to lingering fingertips, a brilliant smile, auburn hair like flames—but no warm flank pressed against him in his bed at night.

Occupied with these thoughts the next day, Raymond used false papers to buy himself a Kawasaki. It was one he could use on a job sooner or later, but right now he needed it as a scout vehicle.

The Western District of Victoria, home to small towns, prime ministers, and old and new money living in National Trust homesteads, lay wide open to the bush bandit. Raymond intended to scout around for a few days, note the banks and the building societies, then strike quickly. He might get lucky. He might earn Vallance's fifty thousand from the first place he hit.

In Geelong he bought maps, then drove southwest, intending to follow the coast to Warrnambool before heading north, then east at Mortlake—a large circle, with plenty of diversions off the beaten track. He'd map the best targets, routes in and out, roadworks, the location of the police stations, areas of traffic congestion, hairpin bends, narrow bridges, school buses. It was painstaking, it was probably obsessive, but Raymond liked to know more than he needed to know before any job.

If he'd not met Vallance, would he have been able to function for much longer as the bush bandit? He knew of only four ways of getting at a bank's holdings—embezzlement, going in with a gang to intercept a large cash transfer, breaking in during a weekend and drilling through to the vault or the safety deposit boxes, or going in alone and armed when the bank was open. Only this last option was open to Raymond. But the banks were getting canny. One day he'd find himself in a trap.

By the fourth day, Raymond was ready to strike.

Biniguy was a small town, no more than a stretch of nondescript public buildings and old, verandahed shops on a country highway that narrowed to form the main street for an eyeblink on the way from Victoria to southeastern South Australia. A small shopping center—with a boutique, a Coles, a bank, a Mitre-10, and a furniture barn built around two sides of a car park—sat behind the main street. From the bank's security point of view, it was a bad location. Raymond listed what was good about it from his point of view: several exits, a public car park right outside, plenty of distracted shoppers around, half a minute from the highway.

He parked the Kawasaki next to an exit at the corner of the supermarket and dismounted. He set off in the opposite direction from the bank, the shotgun stuffed inside the pack on his back. He was interested in the buildings that overlooked the shopping center, in particular a side-street block of flats and the rear of a hall and a public library on the main street. He was looking for a stake-out. There was a good chance of one, after all the outrage he'd precipitated in the past few weeks.

He crossed the street at an angle and entered the flats. All the sounds of the town were cut off inside the foyer. Only his muted breathing sounded in the still, stale air of the stairwell. He listened. He was listening for a cough, the staticky scratch of a hand radio, the rattle of a venetian blind.

Raymond waited for ten minutes, then left the flats and cut across to the external wooden steps behind the hall and adjoining library. He climbed, went in. The windows were opaque, ancient white paint over them. He poked his head around a few doors and along a few dim corridors.

Nothing.

As he descended the stairs he cast about over the car park, looking for other likely police stake-out posts. There was one, an electrician's van near the front door of the bank. But the rear windows were clear, and all he could see in there, a minute later, were tool boxes, switches, and coils of insulated wire. The electrician himself was on a ladder propped against the facia of the boutique, fixing a new neon sign into place. He looked genuine. No radio apparent; no mic or earpiece on a wire. Finally Raymond wandered idly past the shops a couple of times. Still nothing. That left the rooftops, but he couldn't check everything.

Raymond went in. There was one customer, a woman with a

sleeping new baby swaddled to the chin in a pale blanket. He knew that she didn't have to be a woman with a baby but a cop with a doll, but the baby snuffled and bleated so he relaxed by half a degree and marked time with a pen and a withdrawal form.

Three staff: a teller, a young woman standing at a keyboard at the rear, the manager inside a glass booth, tapping the keys of a desk calculator as he flipped through a stack of receipts.

When the woman was gone, Raymond approached the teller. All she could see of his face were his teeth, bared in a distorting grimace, dark glasses, and bike helmet. She was about to point to a sign that told motorcyclists to remove their helmets when her eyes were drawn to the yawning mouth of the shotgun and she whimpered a little.

Raymond said nothing, merely pushed an airlines bag across the counter to her. She began to fill it, from her own till, then used a key to open the neighboring tills. Raymond wondered briefly if she had been held up before. The others hadn't noticed him yet. The keyboard rattled; the manager continued to count his money. Raymond collected the bag from the teller, held his finger to his lips, and saw her eyes look past him and widen in surprise.

He turned. It was a silent world beyond the plate glass, a world where a reversal could appear out of nowhere and you wouldn't know it. A security guard had stationed himself near the door. He was sipping coffee and had his head cranked up to yarn with the electrician.

Raymond said gruffly, "Wasn't here yesterday."

"We have him on rotation with our other branches in the region," the teller said.

Raymond moved quickly. He abandoned the money and the shotgun, stripped off his leather bike jacket and helmet, and walked whistling from the bank. He guessed that he had about thirty seconds before the bank staff gathered their wits. The guard glanced incuriously at him. Raymond left the shopping center on foot and walked to the hospital. He stole an ambulance and drove as far as the next town before entering a system of side roads that would take him east. There were no road blocks and no pursuit cars. There would be soon, but he'd be well out of the area by then.

Later he stole a community bus and drove it to Geelong. There he rented a car. On the drive north to Melbourne, his heart stopped hammering and he said goodbye to the bush bandit. It was done in a second, and in that same second he defined the aims and limitations of his new life. One, he'd no longer hit small targets. No more country towns and their modest banks. Two, he needed one big score that would bankroll his share of the *Eliza Dean* syndicate. Three, he needed a good accomplice.

This time he met Chaffey on a park bench near the Exhibition Building. The glass wall extension gave crisp, out-of-true reflections of the main hall and the gardens, the strolling lovers seemed to yaw and bend like figures in funhouse mirrors.

"I'll do both," Raymond said. "Spring your bloke from remand and lift that collection of paintings."

The fat lawyer tossed a pebble at a pigeon. "Pleased to hear that, son. Steer comes up for trial soon, so he has to be sprung some time in the next few days."

"You said fifteen thousand? Not much for the risk involved."

"Take it or leave it, son. This isn't a cheap operation. Your role is only part of it. There's also his new ID, a safe passage out of the country, the dosh to tide him over till he's settled. There's whatever gear you and his girlfriend decide is needed. There's a new ID and a ticket out for her as well."

"All right, all right, I get the picture, I'll do it for the fifteen. You said up front?"

"Up front, but only for this job."

It was a step down in Raymond's career and he felt obscurely ashamed. It wasn't the kind of job Wyatt would line up for.

"These paintings," he said.

"Time's running out for that, too. Not this weekend but the weekend after. Two days when the collection will be off the walls and in storage and the alarm system turned off while they renovate." Chaffey turned his massive head to watch a girl walk by. "Like I said, it's a two-man job. You found someone?"

"My uncle comes to mind."

Chaffey went still. Then he tossed another pebble. "Heard something about him during the week that doesn't exactly inspire confidence."

"Like what?"

"He tried to flog some precious stones back to an insurance company and almost got caught by the cops."

Raymond felt the pull of conflicting emotions. He could picture his uncle's nerve and style, but why hadn't Wyatt told him about the botched handover, had a laugh about it with him, if nothing else? They were family, after all.

And did Wyatt still have the stones?

"But he didn't get caught."

"True, true," Chaffey said.

"Plus he's stolen paintings before," Raymond said. "Art, stuff like that, it's not my thing."

He recreated his apartment in his head. Half a dozen prints he'd rented, along with the furniture.

"See if you can arrange a meeting," Chaffey said.

Have to find him first, Raymond thought. He coughed and said, "About the prison break."

"Yes?"

"Keep it between you and me. My uncle doesn't need to know about it."

Chaffey swung his huge head around. Raymond felt the force of the man's hard gaze. Men like Chaffey saw corruption every day. It corrupted them, gave a corrupt spin to their insights.

"You mean he wouldn't approve," Chaffey said finally, and Raymond would quite happily have strangled Chaffey then.

Chapter 15

Chaffey called in favors and made promises and when Steer was finally moved to the remand center in Sunshine he made the trip out there by taxi. The place was privately run and tried to kid itself that plenty of bright fresh paint and natural light, and its situation alongside other public buildings, placed it at the cutting edge of modern incarceration practice, but Chaffey wasn't fooled. There was no concealing the rifles and batons, the commerce in drugs, phonecards and cigarettes, the stench of hopelessness, and hate the moment you got through the main door.

Still, he'd rather have a consultation with Steer in the remand center than in Pentridge, where the interview rooms were grim and spare, the walls always cold to the touch, the high windows too smeared and deepset to catch the light, the air always ringing with the smack of metal against metal.

Steer, they said, was helping the maintenance crew. There'd be a thirty-minute wait. Chaffey mentally added another thirty to that and asked to see the paperwork on his client.

The clerk sighed elaborately. "You want it now?"

Chaffey was used to grudging prison staff. One, he was a lawyer, he had it easy. He didn't have to be shut up with the dregs of society for hours at a time. Two, lawyers, like cops, kept things to themselves. They looked at a bloke's file and their little minds ticked over and they went off and did important things. They were right up themselves. Three, Chaffey looked rich and fat. Four, he didn't wear a uniform. Chaffey read all of these things in the sour face of the clerk, not necessarily in that order.

The man put him in a smoky side room. A transistor radio vibrated on a window shelf, a poorly tuned talkback host encouraging every vicious prejudice ever thought or uttered. Two guards came in, made coffee, stared at Chaffey, yelled above the racketing radio, went out again. Chaffey knew that he was being put in his place. He didn't care. It was all in their heads, not his.

The officer came back with Steer's file. Apparently Steer was behaving himself. Well, he would be, given that he intended to escape on the one hand and was looking at long gaol time if that fell through on the other.

Fifty minutes later, Chaffey was taken to an interview room. Steer sat on a plastic chair at a plastic table, blowing smoke rings at the ceiling.

Chaffey turned to the guard. "My client and I would like some privacy, if you don't mind."

The man flushed. "No skin off my nose."

He left. Chaffey said, "Are we okay in here?"

Steer nodded. "Cost me fifty smackers. No one's listening."

"Good," Chaffey said.

He made a rapid assessment of his client. Steer was watchful, careful, apparently relaxed and self-contained. "Keeps to himself," the report said. "The hard men of the yard leave him alone."

Chaffey could see why. You sensed the glittering danger in him, just as you sensed it in certain dogs.

"I've seen Denise," Chaffey began.

Steer nodded. He tipped back his throat and huffed three smoke rings at the spitting fluorescent tube.

Chaffey saw his teeth then: gaol-rotted teeth, full of stumps and black cavities. "We're ready to roll, our end," he said. "New Zealand passports and driver's licenses, a boat from Lakes Entrance to a freighter, a guy to drive you."

"Who?"

"His name is Ray Wyatt. The police don't know him. Good nerve, cautious, he won't let you down. Denise has been working on your shopping list. The rest is up to you."

"Things are jake my end," Steer said. "Back up a bit. This guy, you say his name is Wyatt?"

Chaffey nodded, adding a chin to the chins that hung over the knot of his tie. "You know him?"

Steer shook his head. "Has he got a father, a nasty piece of work, knocks over payroll vans and that?"

Chaffey thought that "nasty piece of work" pretty well described Steer. "The lad's uncle. Is that a problem?"

Steer smiled. There was no humor or good will in it. "Just asking."

"Now, about your money," Chaffey said.

Two hundred thousand dollars, in a fireproof steel floor-safe at his house, cemented into a hole in the corner of his basement. Steer's money, and Steer knew the combination, just in case, but that two hundred grand still burnt a hole in Chaffey's head. He was not mug enough to touch it, though. Steer would slice him open and whistle "Waltzing Matilda" while he did it.

"What about my money? You fucking lost it at the casino?"

"Keep your shirt on," Chaffey said. "It's in the basement

where it's always been. As soon as you're settled somewhere, I'll wire it to you."

"That you will," Steer said, reaching to stub out his cigarette on the table, just millimeters away from Chaffey's soft, fat, pink, well-tended hand.

Chapter 16

Wyatt always kept an emergency bag packed. Within minutes of killing Frank Jardine's brother, he'd left another stage of his life behind him.

A new bolthole. He couldn't stay in Hobart. There was the mainland, but too many people knew him there, too many wanted him dead. He'd risk short, hit-and-run visits to the capital cities, but it would be inviting trouble to base himself in one of them.

And so Wyatt drove north, in a Magna rented using a false set of papers. He took the Midland Highway. Wind gusts rocked the car in the high country after Hobart, where the road narrowed and levelled out for the dreary stretch up through the center of the state. Traffic was sparse and slow and inclined to be careless. Wyatt found himself tensing at the wheel. The long hours and the strain of his life brought sharp aches to his neck and shoulders.

A new bolthole, and a big score to build up his cash reserves. That meant working with someone again. Wyatt thought about his nephew's proposition. He counted the advantages again. One,

Raymond was family and seemed to look up to him. Two, Raymond had successfully planned and pulled a number of armed holdups. Three, he'd never been caught. Four, he wasn't a junkie. The boy probably had vices and weaknesses, but they weren't apparent, and they hadn't got in the way of his bank raids.

Something else was prompting Wyatt, a feeling that lacked clear definition but connected Raymond with the child who had stepped into the traffic, inviting death. His brother's son. Raymond was the son of a weak, vicious man, and Wyatt had done nothing to make things better.

The road wound through valleys and rich farmland. The headlights flared over roadsigns that portrayed fat sheep and historic towns. He saw convict-built stonewall fences and imposing gates that indicated fine homesteads set back amongst English trees. He was in Tasmania's conservative heartland. The seat of government was in the south but the old money was in the north and it ruled the upper house of government.

At one o'clock he pulled off the road and slept until dawn. He was no more than thirty minutes from Devonport, but he knew that he'd attract suspicion if he tried to rent a room this early in the morning.

He drove to the next town, locked the car and walked to a café. Smells of toast and coffee inside; a couple of bleary farmers and truckies at a corner table. He ate, walked for an hour, drove on.

Later that morning he rented a holiday flat in Devonport. It was a depressing place. The window of the main room overlooked a block of similar flats—the Astor Apartments, pale yellow brick, rusting wrought iron, rotted window sills—and leaked a weak grey light into the place. Low, pebbled ceiling, wiry carpets the consistency of a kitchen scourer, Aborigines on black velvet in wooden frames on the walls. Frayed, burnt-orange armchairs and sofa. Parents came here exhausted with their tribes of children every summer and found little rest. They existed on fish and chips and videos. Humankind herded together in disappointment and conflict until death, Wyatt thought. He thought of Liz Redding and wondered at his own fate.

That afternoon he went out for maps, tourist brochures and real estate listings. He spent the afternoon poring over them and making phone calls. He gave himself a week. When he stared out of the window, early that evening, he saw the running lights of the ferry as it set out for Melbourne, sliding massively down the channel toward the open sea, its superstructure dwarfing the little houses and cheap holiday flats.

In the end, he didn't need a week. Three days later, Wyatt moved to a remote wooden house near Flowerdale on the north coast, with a view across abrupt small hills to a slice of Bass Strait. It was a region of orchards, tree nurseries, dairy farms, creeks, gorges and muddy tracks. No one was likely to question him in such a place. It was a rental house and renters had always stayed a while there, working or not working, maybe bludging on the welfare system, maybe teaching in the local school for a few terms. Wyatt was just another one of them.

Chapter 17

Liz Redding didn't get to Hobart. Her suspension was made official, and she was obliged to report every day, pending an inquiry. She might have slipped away regardless of that, but Gosse called her into his office and told her that they'd had a call from the Tasmania Police.

He drummed his fingers on his desk. "The name Jardine mean anything to you?"

"You've read my report, sir."

"Indeed I have. Your friend Wyatt worked with a man called Frank Jardine."

"Not my friend, sir."

Gosse ignored her. "This Jardine has—or rather, *had*—a brother."

"I wouldn't know, sir."

"Wouldn't you? Well, the brother has turned up dead—stabbed—in a flat in Battery Point, down in Hobart. Needless to say, being a resident of Melbourne, it wasn't his flat."

So that's what Nettie meant, Liz thought. "Whose flat was it, sir?"

"That's the interesting part, Sergeant. The tenant was a man, no one knew him, the name probably false, nothing left to identify him, no prints, wiped clean."

Liz sat stonily watching Gosse.

"That photograph we have of Wyatt. It's not very clear, but the real estate agent who let the flat to this man positively identifies him."

What did Gosse want from her? He was playing some kind of game, loading a lot of meaning between the lines. Liz said, "So, he's on the run, sir. I hope you catch him."

Gosse snapped forward across the empty desk. She smelt toothpaste and coffee. He said, "Did you warn him, Sergeant?"

She stared at a point above his shoulder. "Sir, I've talked to the Association lawyer. If you want to charge me, charge me. If you want to find evidence against me, go out and find it. Meanwhile, all I'm guilty of is being too dedicated to my job, working outside of regulations in the interest of bringing a crooked copper to justice. That's all I'm admitting to, that's all I've done. Either throw the book at me or sack me or reinstate me. Until then, I've said all I'm obliged to say."

Gosse rubbed his ring finger vigorously over his forehead. The movement made him grimace, as though he were screaming silently. Liz thought of Wyatt, who had probably been the killer. Self defense? She hoped so. Wyatt didn't have the empty moral center of a thrill killer. Anyway, not the Wyatt she'd known on the yacht.

"Fuck this," Gosse said. He hunted in his side drawer, slid a form across the desk toward her. "A warrant to search your house."

Liz let the anger burn coldly. "You won't find anything. Plenty of knickers, in case you want to have a sniff."

"You may accompany us. You may even have the Association rep present if you so desire."

"That won't be necessary. But I'll be watching you, you bastard, every step of the way."

An hour later she was sitting, seething, in an armchair by the window, as Gosse, two other detectives and two uniformed constables searched her flat. She knew there was nothing to find. There was also nothing they could plant, unless Gosse had somehow got hold of the remaining rings and necklaces from the Asahi Collection, or something that belonged to Wyatt.

A third constable stayed in the room with her, standing uncomfortably by the door.

"Sit down," Liz said.

He blushed. He was young and pimpled. "I'm right, thanks."

"Suit yourself."

She watched gloomily as one of the detectives searched the room. He looked inside the CD cases and magazines, shook vases, tapped the fireplace tiles with his knuckles. He even took a screwdriver to the gas heater. It was dusty. He rocked back on his heels, sneezing.

Where would you hide a fortune in rings, bracelets, necklaces and tiaras if you were Wyatt and on the run and needing to travel light? Her thinking brought her by degrees to the yacht. Where on the yacht had the jewels been hidden in the first place, before Wyatt ran with them?

She straightened involuntarily, coughed to mask it, relaxed again. Three o'clock. Gosse would want to question her again at ten the next morning. Plenty of time.

At 3:30 Gosse said, "That's all for now, Sergeant. Thank you."

Liz said, putting on the sweetness, "Find anything? That earring I lost last year? A ten cent piece down the back of the sofa? Maybe a letter from my old Gran I forgot to answer?"

"Tomorrow morning, ten sharp," Gosse said.

When they were gone, Liz left through her back door, climbed the fence into the alley, and made her way to a taxi stand two blocks away. She told the driver to take her to the Budget place in Elizabeth Street, where she rented a Corolla, and by 5:15 she was on the foreshore at Hastings.

It looked different. Then again, everything had been distorted the first time—dawn, the aftermath of a storm, her groggy head.

She found the yacht tied to a berth amongst a lot of small, flashy weekend yachts. There was a crime-scene tape around the rail. She looked about her. The place was closing for the day. She stepped over the tape and climbed down the steps to the area beneath the deck.

The yacht had been baking in the sun for days. The air below smelt of vinyl and glue, close and stale.

She started with the cabins, and worked her way along. By the time she got to the galley her hands were dirty, her fingernails torn.

She found the safe by accident. She was leaning her weight on the wall oven, resting, thinking, and when she stepped back she heard the soft click of a spring lock. The oven had moved a little, the edge jutting out a few millimeters from the wall. Liz hooked her sore fingers on the lip and pulled.

The oven slid out silently on well-greased channels, rather like a drawer in a modern kitchen. There was a space behind it. Liz reached into the wall cavity and the bulky, black felt bundle she brought into the light fell open and poured a stream of vivid stones and cool gold settings onto the carpet at her feet. The gold gleamed, the faceted stones flashed the colors of the spectrum. "Oh," she said aloud.

Liz Redding dated the permanent seal on the shift in her view of the world, and of herself, to this moment. She felt the tug of the stones. Her head filled with risky impulses. Her heart beat. Her mouth was dry. She wanted to walk further into the edgy darkness enjoyed by a man like Wyatt.

Chapter 18

The safe house was a boxy weatherboard perched on a steep slope above a creek in Warrandyte, in the ranges north of Melbourne. Raymond felt claustrophobic, shut in by the dense overhang of trees, the squabbling birds, the gullies and hills. You could see for miles from his balcony in the city. Here all you could see was the fence through the trees in the garden, then more trees. If you were lucky you got a glimpse of the sky. Otherwise there was only the house and the driveway and his Jag.

And Denise Meickle, waiting stonily outside the front door. Raymond nodded, approached, not liking what he saw. He was supposed to spend a few days with her, help her bloke get out of remand, hang around afterward and help both of them get out of the country? For fifteen thousand bucks? Jesus. He wouldn't be listing this on his CV.

Raymond got closer. Denise Meickle was a real sadsack, okay clothes but gloomy in the face, with the kind of skin that is permanently red and chapped around the mouth and nostrils.

Hefty jaw, broad forehead, slight body, as though her head and her trunk belonged to different people. It was inevitable that Raymond would think about Allie Roden and begin to count his luck. Steer had to be really hard-up.

"Made it," he said.

The Meickle woman looked at her watch. "I was expecting you an hour ago."

No wonder Chaffey hadn't wanted to be in on their first meeting. "I got lost," Raymond said.

He'd taken a winding route through Doncaster and Templestowe, gazing unbelievingly at the crass houses, the evidence of vulgar new wealth, a lot of it acquired dishonestly. There'd been a story going around a few years ago that Wyatt had tangled with a crime family out here, raided their compound for the money they owed him. Nerve and vision. Raymond felt a kind of envy and resentment stir inside him. Why would Wyatt want to help him lift a collection of paintings, especially if he had a million bucks' worth of stolen jewels hidden away? There had to be cash stowed away, too, over the years. Wyatt could pick and choose as he liked. *One day they'll say the same about me*, Raymond thought.

"Tricky place to find," he said now, "tucked away back here in the hills."

Meickle grunted. "You might as well come inside. Bring your bag with you."

Raymond followed her into the house. It smelt of treated baltic pine, wood stain, and a stale trace of cat. It belonged to friends of Denise Meickle. They were overseas for a year. Meickle had a key, but wasn't expected to do more than water the garden every few days.

They came to a poky loungeroom with a glass wall that faced a stand of spindly tall gums. Raymond waited, content to let

Meickle take the lead. According to Chaffey, she used to be a Correctional Services psychologist at Ararat Prison, where she met Steer. She might be a gloomy, box-faced cow but Raymond knew that a psychologist is someone who reads your mind, so he intended to keep his trap shut as much as possible.

"Sleeping arrangements," she said. "I'm in the main bedroom, you're through here."

She led him to a tiny bedroom. There was a single bed, a nursery frieze around three of the walls, a zoo poster taped to an inbuilt wardrobe, a window that looked upon more fucking trees. "Uh huh," he said.

"If you don't like it, there's the sofa."

"This will do."

"When you're ready, we can start work."

Raymond unpacked. He found her in the kitchen, watching moodily as an electric kettle boiled. She poured weak coffee and they sat at a chrome and laminex kitchen table, 1960s kitsch. Raymond stretched the kinks out of his back and shoulders, yawned, and said, "I suggest we start with—"

It was clear that Denise harbored all of the disappointments of her thirty years in her face and her voice. The face was pinched and disapproving, the voice, too: "You start by getting a few things straight. First, you're here to help out, not take charge, not do your own thing, just do as you're told, okay?"

"That's cool."

"The plan is Tony's and mine. We—"

It was odd hearing Steer's first name. "Big Tone," Raymond said, then wondered why he'd said it.

"None of this is a joke. You come recommended by Chaffey, but I've yet to be convinced. You don't impress me. You don't make me laugh. You don't turn me on. I'm not going to cook or clean for you. Got all that?"

Delivered with a low, uninflected voice full of authority. Raymond saluted. "Yes, sir, ma'am, sir."

She waited. She might have been counting to ten. *This is an awfully small house*, Raymond thought, *to be holed up in with a whaddaya call it, femo-nazi.*

"The plan," Denise Meickle said, "is that we get him out on Sunday."

"Bit soonish," Raymond said.

"It happens to be a long weekend. The benefits are as follows. First, the remand center in Sunshine is understaffed anyway, but even more so when we factor in the long weekend. Secondly, he's in a unit looked after by female officers."

Raymond clicked his tongue approvingly. "They're not likely to try it on. Pushovers."

"In other circumstances," Denise said, "I'd take exception to that. But you're right, they'll be easier to control if anything goes wrong for Tony on the inside. Just two female officers in charge of a unit of twenty inmates."

"What time?"

"Six in the evening. Just getting dark out. Inside they'll be finishing dinner, heading off to watch TV. Everyone milling around, relaxed, a fair bit of noise and orderly confusion."

Raymond gazed out at the thick trees. Trees for miles. Houses and towns, too, and hills and paddocks, but this house was set fair in the middle of a fucking forest, it seemed like. He'd go mad if he didn't go out occasionally. But what really burned him up was the thought that if he didn't come up with some big money as a deposit soon, Vallance would sell the last syndicate share to someone else. The fifteen grand from this job would only appease Vallance for a while. What he really needed was to find Wyatt and convince him to help out with Chaffey's art theft.

He turned to Denise. "You haven't said how."

"Wait here."

She came back with an architect's drawing, which she rolled out on the table, weighing both ends down with their empty cups. She had short fingers with unflattering nails—white flecked, poorly trimmed. Raymond liked a woman who looked after her hands. Allie's slim hands on his back, Denise Meickle's little hands on Steer's back. He shook the image away and tried to concentrate.

"This is the wall facing the alley that runs off Craigie Street. It's all administration here on the first floor. This—" she tapped a small rectangular shape "—is an air-conditioning unit set in the wall. It looks as if it can't be moved but in fact it will slide right out once Tony undoes a bolt holding it to the wall."

"How's he going to do that?"

"Every air-conditioner in the building was serviced recently. Tony was on the work detail because he's good with machinery and electrics. When he replaced this particular unit he made sure it looked finished off but in reality it will slide right away from the wall, leaving a gap he can climb through."

"So we park in the alley and pick him up."

"Yes."

"Stolen car?"

"We steal two cars, and two sets of plates for them. One car to pick him up. We drive it a short distance to the first change-over car, somewhere near the start of the Hume Freeway, then somewhere half an hour out of Melbourne we change cars again, using my car to head across back here to Warrandyte. They'll think we're heading north, into New South Wales."

"I steal the cars, I drive?"

"It's one of the things you're supposed to be good at."

"I'm good," Raymond said simply. "Where do you come into the picture?"

"I'll pick you up on the Hume. I've also been shopping for the gear."

"What gear?"

Denise slid a sheet of notepaper across the table. "Shopping list."

"Jesus Christ," Raymond said.

Stun gun, mobile phones, camping gear, camouflage net, police scanners, Victoria Police radio codes, handcuffs, bolt cutters, three pistols, three shotguns, ammunition, food, petrol and water.

"How we supposed to get all this stuff?"

"Most of it I've taken care of already."

"Stun gun?"

"Mail order from the States. Arrived a couple of days ago."

"Jesus."

Raymond thought: *This is how the hard boys operate. Look and learn, Raymond, old son.* "Why all the outdoor stuff?"

"If something goes wrong we'll head for the bush."

Christ, Raymond thought. *Mosquitoes, rabbits, foxes, sleeping with a rock in the small of your back, wiping your arse with a bunch of leaves.* "A lot of stuff to buy."

"I need you to buy some of it, like the phones, camping equipment, etcetera. The rest is taken care of."

"Must have some cluey mates."

"You'll be told what you need to know, Ray. Don't worry about it."

For all her mousy ways, she was pretty confident. "I'm not worried," Raymond said.

"Good." She looked at him, and he could see that she was looking for a way to make him feel that he was just as much at the center of the operation as she was. "Um, how will you get the cars?"

Raymond thought, *stupid bitch*, then leaned back in his chair. "We want cars that won't be missed until several hours after we break Steer out. We're looking at people who take a train to the city mid-Sunday afternoon—off to a movie, maybe a part-time job, concert, whatever."

"Good thinking."

Raymond nodded.

"Make sure one of them is a four-wheel-drive. Tough. Good tires."

"How come?"

"In case we have to leave the Hume and head into the bush."

Always a step ahead of him. Raymond pushed back from the table. "No time like the present. Got any cash?"

Meickle frowned. "Chaffey's given you fifteen thousand."

"My fee," Raymond said. "It doesn't go on expenses."

Grumbling, she counted five hundred dollars into his hand. "I want receipts."

Raymond took the Ruger automatic and a suppressor, stowed them in the glove box of the Jag, and headed down to the city to go shopping. He started with the camping shops in Elizabeth Street. It felt good buying the best, peeling off fifties and hundreds of Denise Meickle's hard-earned cash.

By six o'clock he'd bought everything on the list. Meickle was expecting him back at the safe house, but she could wait. Raymond let himself into his flat at 6:15, showered and shaved, and was ready for the voice on the intercom at 6:30.

"Come on up."

He opened the door naked. It wasn't something you could do with every bird, but somehow he knew that Allie Roden wasn't likely to scream and run.

She didn't.

Chapter 19

By six o'clock on the eighteenth, the two escape vehicles were in place. Raymond, armed with an automatic pistol for himself and another for Steer, and wearing gloves and a balaclava, nosed a stolen Fairmont into the alley next to the remand center and waited. Shortly after six o'clock, Steer came feetfirst through the wall and dropped lightly to the ground.

Those aspects of the plan were faultless. The first thing to come unravelled was the drive away from the remand center. Raymond was barrelling the Fairmont out of the alley, braking for Craigie Street, when a taxi drew in to drop off a passenger and he braked but slid smack into the side of the cab.

"Get out," Steer said, waving his revolver at Raymond. "*Move.*"

The Fairmont was undrivable, the bumper and wing folded in against the right front tire.

"The taxi," Steer said.

Raymond followed him. The Fairmont had smashed in both passenger-side doors of the taxi, so Steer headed around to the driver's side. Raymond found himself matching Steer move for move. Steer opened the driver's door and hauled out the cabbie; Raymond opened the rear door and hauled out the passenger, who waved a wallet at him angrily.

"Stop daydreaming," Steer screamed. "Get in, for Christ's sake, and drive like the clappers."

Raymond followed Steer into the front of the taxi. He felt a kind of elation, a kind of decisive, get-out-of-my-way competence. It was the feeling he got when he walked into a bank with the shotgun. He yanked the lever into drive and peeled away.

Raymond was soaring now. He slipped the taxi rapidly through the sluggish Sunday traffic and onto a broad, deserted avenue. Here his exhilaration broke. "Ha!" he shouted, punching the wheel. "Yes!"

Steer's big hand seemed to float free of his lap and suddenly swing like an axe against Raymond's upper lip. His head rocked back. The pain was intense and blood spurted from his mouth.

"There's a certain bone in the nose. Hit a certain way, it gets driven into the brain. Not a good way to die. So don't fuck up again. Fuck up again and you're history."

Raymond eyed Steer bitterly. The guy was like Wyatt, a bit long in the tooth but coldly dedicated, efficient in the way he moved, full of power like a coiled spring. "How was I to know—"

"You didn't look," Steer said. "You just barged through."

Raymond fished for a handkerchief and spat into it. Street lights slipped past outside and he wondered what he was doing here with this psychopath. Steer seemed to fill the car, heavy and accusatory, so that Raymond couldn't help himself. He had to appease the man. "Go all right inside?"

"Just drive."

They switched to the Range Rover at Thomastown. Raymond felt rattled, and at the entrance to the Hume Freeway accelerated ahead of a truck. He sensed the driver behind them pushing his brakes to the floor. Headlights flooded them and a horn sounded, mournful in the night.

"Easy, pal," Steer said. "No sense getting us killed."

Raymond relaxed. The bastard seemed easier with him now. He drove on into the black night. After a while Steer muttered, "I hear you're Wyatt's nephew."

Raymond said hastily, "He doesn't know about this."

"Good," Steer said. "The fewer the better. You'll be sticking around for a couple of days, right?"

"Yes."

Steer seemed to relax, stretching his legs and settling his shoulder against the door. "Not many of us around any more. The old school, me and your uncle. It's all drugs with the youngsters now. No finesse. Too impatient to plan. It's a skill. You take each job slowly, meticulously. You have to think it through."

"Right," Raymond said.

"Like, never set up a base in the same town as the target. If you're working with others, you each make a solo reconnaissance of the target. Stay in motels or overnight vans in caravan parks. Never let yourself get boxed in. Make sure your alternative escape routes are clear—no roadworks, no rubbish bins. If it's going to help, tie up emergency services with a fire or an explosion somewhere."

Steer was on automatic pilot, lecturing, maybe out of nervousness. Still, Raymond told himself, why the fuck do I have to listen to it? He said sharply, "You're not telling me anything I don't already know."

Steer shrugged. "Chill out, Sunshine. No offense. Only you'd be surprised at the number of amateurs, addicts, and ego merchants there are in this game."

Raymond could almost taste the dislike in his mouth. "So, how do you know I'm not one of them?"

Steer went very still, very concentrated, a chill in his soft voice: "You come recommended, but if you fuck me around, remember that I've got a lot of favors owing. I know things. I network. The moment I walk into a nick, I run it. I know things or can find them out, and I'd track you down and not even your famous uncle could save you."

They drove into the night. After a while, Steer rubbed his hands together. "How'd you get on with my bird?"

"Fine," Raymond said warily. Had the bastard been stewing away in remand, wondering if Denise was screwing around on him? He waved a reassuring hand. "I mean, we were pretty busy doing our own thing, putting this together."

Steer breathed in and out heavily. "She's an ace chick. I've really been looking forward to this."

Christ, Raymond thought. *The bastard's actually keen on her.*

Half an hour later they met Denise in a shadowy parking bay on the Hume Freeway. Denise flung herself onto Steer and Raymond had to stand back for a while, his head averted, while they kissed and murmured.

When they were finished, he said, "Don't want to be hanging around here much longer."

"Time for a quick snap?" Denise asked.

Raymond frowned. "What are you on about?"

Denise pulled a small camera from her bag and said, self-consciously, "A record of this historic moment."

"Jesus," Raymond said.

But he was taken with the idea. First he snapped Denise and Steer with their arms around each other, then Denise snapped Raymond with Steer.

Then the job unravelled again. "People," Steer announced, "I've got things I need to do. I'll see you at the house sometime tomorrow morning."

Denise had been hanging onto his arm, dopey with love, but stiffened when she heard this. "What things?"

"I'll explain later. Just till lunchtime tomorrow. I want both of you to stay put at the safe house till I get there."

Raymond said, "This wasn't part of the original plan."

Steer began to advance on him. Raymond stood his ground, trying not to flinch from the chest pressing against his, the hot breath gusting into his face. "I said, I'll be back, okay?" A finger jabbed him. "You got that? You're paid to see it through to the end."

Raymond said nothing, just watched coldly as Steer climbed into the Range Rover, but Denise disintegrated. She cried out, even clawed at Steer's door as he drove away. When he was gone, she fell to her knees, shoulders heaving. "Where's he going? Why's he doing this to me?"

Raymond walked across to her and helped her stand. "Come on, we have to get out of here."

"What will I do? What if he never comes back? I can't go back to work. I can't go home. They'll arrest me. What will I do?"

Drive me fucking nuts for a start, Raymond thought.

Chapter 20

Information was everything. Whenever Steer found himself in new environments or unknown company he put out feelers, made bargains, traded and exerted influence and pressure. Within hours of being arrested, he'd known who had sold him to the jacks. It was an outfitter called Phil Gent. You needed guns, explosives and detonators, a car, mobile phone, walkie talkies? Speak to Gent. Well, Gent had outfitted Steer's latest job, a warehouse load of Scotch, only one nightwatchman to deal with, then gone and spilled it to the jacks, who'd been waiting when Steer came out.

Steer had never met Gent at home. It was always on neutral ground such as a pub, a motel room or the docks. Within a couple of hours of his admission to Pentridge, he'd learnt where Gent lived: in a farmhouse near Colac in the Western District.

Steer headed there after leaving Raymond and Denise. Wyatt's nephew had looked pissed off, Denise heartbroken. It wasn't a betrayal, Steer intended to come back again, but it must have looked odd.

He thought about betrayal as he drove through the night. He'd been stiffed by Wyatt once, but right now he was more interested in Gent. What was it that made Gent sell him to the cops? For that matter, why had blokes in prison sold Gent to him?

To dog, to grass, to inform, to dob in. Steer tried to analyze it as the white line unfolded ahead of his headlights and darkness held him alone in the night. You'd do it for gain, like money, influence, power, advantage. You'd do it for revenge. You'd do it to get someone off your back. You'd do it to stop something from happening.

Steer wondered about the other side of the equation. Take the cop who gave his ear to Gent: he'd have to reward Gent in some way, like give him money or turn a blind eye. There was dependency in that kind of relationship. Did the cop hate it? Not that he could afford to pin all his hopes on one informant. Someone like Gent might get cold feet or want more out of the deal or stop hearing good information if whispers about his reliability got about.

Or, Steer thought, smirking, someone like Gent might simply stop breathing.

It was a puzzle to Steer how Gent was able to live with himself. Money and favors would help, but he'd still have to come to terms with the fact that he was a dog. Did the shame and guilt get to him, or did he make the treachery acceptable to himself with a bit of fancy rationalizing?—like: "I'm doing this to those who deserve it. I'm not hurting those who haven't hurt me."

On and on, the black road renewed itself in the light of the moon and the headlights. There was another form of treachery that could not be rationalized. It boiled down to abandoning your partners on a job, letting them take the risks and get caught by the law. Mostly it could be explained by greed, impulse or cowardice, but when a man like Wyatt does it to you it's cold and hard and calculated and unforgivable.

On the approach road to Gent's farmhouse, Steer turned off his headlights and kept the engine revs down. Gent might be naturally jumpy, or he might have heard about the prison break on the evening news. Either way, Steer didn't want Gent to know he was there until it was too late. The house came into view, an old weatherboard set well back from the road, looking grey and unlovely in the poor light of the moon. Steer pulled to the grass verge, switched off, and got out.

There was a kelpie on a mat outside the back door. It bared its teeth, it might even have attacked, but it didn't bark. Steer shot it through the head.

A light came on inside the house. Then a shape appeared at the window, Gent leaning to peer into the darkness. Steer shot him through the glass.

Steer stood where he was for a while, blinking, trying to encourage vision back into his eyes. Shows what a man can forget. His old training—unless you want to blind yourself for a couple of minutes, never look at the muzzle flash of a gun at night.

The darkness around him remained still and silent. When he could see again, Steer walked to the broken window and looked in.

Gent lay dying on his back. Typical gut-shot symptoms—grey face, glassy eyes, labored breathing, a pleading grimace that heralded death. Then Gent retched violently, a froth of dark blood spilling from his mouth. His eyes widened. His tongue protruded. Steer turned away. He knew the final stage well enough. Gent would turn blue-grey, the cast of death.

Steer considered hiding the body. Kick in the teeth first, burn the hands, dump the body in a gorge somewhere. Unidentifiable remains, the papers would say. But the time, the trouble, the cleaning up the house first, the removal of the kelpie—stuff that for a joke.

Instead, Steer went into the house and ransacked it, making

it look like an aggravated burglary. And he found five hundred bucks in an envelope taped to the bottom of a drawer, so that was all right, plus four grand and a passport in a cavity behind a false power point in a skirting board in the bedroom. The passport was no good to him, for Gent had the squashed features and jowls of a bulldog, and Chaffey had supplied him with a new ID, but the cash would come in handy.

Finally Steer concealed the Range Rover in a barn at the rear of the house. Gent owned a Kombi, parked under a tree in the yard. It needed plenty of choke and was low on fuel. Steer thought about that.

What stopped him thinking was the torch, a finger of light coming slowly across the flat ground behind the house, and an elderly woman's voice quavering, "Mr. Gent? Are you all right?"

Steer started the Kombi and drove slowly out of the yard. He hadn't seen another house nearby, but clearly there was one. Maybe the old dear would turn around and go home again, thinking she'd heard a backfire, but he couldn't take that chance. He'd have to find another car, and he'd have to take a different route out, a longer one, deep into the Western District then maybe north to the goldfield country. He'd allow himself two days, otherwise he'd be too late to meet the freighter off Lakes Entrance.

As he weaved through the Western District he thought about Denise. She loved him. It was gratifying. There hadn't been much love in his life. Denise wasn't exactly an oil painting, a bit pink and dampish and sour at the world, but she had a good brain. In fact, she made him feel obscurely inadequate. He wanted her to admire him; otherwise there would be that niggling doubt—was she just another female getting her kicks from screwing a hard man?

And Steer thought about Raymond Wyatt, a bit of luck that had just fallen into his lap.

At dawn the next morning he watched a farmer wave goodbye

to his wife outside a log-cabin kit house and drive off in a dual-cab ute. There was a barrelly Falcon in the carport attached to the house, and no kids' clothing on the Hill's Hoist in the backyard. Steer gave the woman a concussive blow to the temple, concealed the Kombi, and drove off in the Falcon ute. At lunchtime he stole a Holden, that evening another Falcon. All the time he was heading west, toward South Australia. At Dimboola he stole a Mazda, fitted it with plates from a scrapyard, and doubled back, driving through the night in heavy rain until he was in the Western District again, closing in on Geelong.

He wasn't expecting the roadblock. He was on a rain-lashed plain and saw brake lights ahead of him through the wash of the wiper blades. Pulling in behind a line of cars and farm vehicles, he thought *roadworks*, but when a muddy ute ahead of him U-turned out of the line and two motorcycle cops flashed past to intercept, he knew that this was no roadworks. He ran a mental eye over himself, over the car. The pistol was in the glove box, in a small tool kit.

He watched his wing mirror. The cops had stopped the ute. The driver, an elderly woman in overalls and rubber boots, climbed out, a kelpie butting through to the ground ahead of her. The woman began to berate the cops. One of them laughed. The other walked to the rear of her ute and searched under the tonneau cover. He apparently found nothing, but noted her plate number and a moment later waved her off.

Why here? Steer thought. *Are they looking for me all over the state?* The van ahead of him moved forward a car length, then stopped. Steer moved with it. The car behind him moved.

He looked at his watch. 9:20. He'd missed the nine o'clock news and would have to wait until ten.

Five minutes later he reached the roadblock, which consisted of three pursuit cars angled so that quick acceleration forward was impossible. Half a dozen cops. Two further motorcycles.

A face filled his window; eyes the color of slate gazed hard at him. Steer tensed, but there was no change in the man's expression, nothing to betray recognition or action. "Your license and registration, please, sir."

"What's going on?" Steer asked, knowing that everyone would ask it.

"Your papers, sir, if you please."

Steer fished the papers Chaffey had given him out of the glove box. He itched to bring out the pistol.

The cop passed the false papers back to him. "Would you open the boot, please, sir?"

Steer leaned down and operated the boot release. There was a faint clunk as the lock disengaged. He turned to watch the cop, who stood to one side and gingerly, with his forefinger, raised the lid. An overnight bag of nondescript clothing, that's all.

The cop shut the boot and returned to the driver's window. "On holiday, are we, sir? From New Zealand?"

"Lousy weather," Steer said. "Might as well be back home."

The cop stood back from the window. "I wonder if you would mind pulling off the road, sir, over there where those other drivers have parked."

"What for?"

"Just routine, sir, if you don't mind."

Steer saw two cars in the mud behind the pursuit cars. He guessed that he shared physical characteristics with both drivers. He started the car, moved forward off the road, switched off. The rain bucketed down. It was miserable, drenching rain, that seemed to reduce the world to the dimensions of a phone box. Figures blurred in the drifting curtain of water, and Steer removed the interior light bulb, pocketed the pistol, opened the passenger door, and walked into the rain and out of the police net.

Chapter 21

His overnight bag lay packed ready to go on the bed. Wyatt stripped off his clothes and went into the bathroom. He prepared the way by hacking the hair from the crown of his head with a pair of scissors. When the bulk was gone he took up the razor, a cheap gadget with a high whine that seemed to cut at the nerves behind his eyeballs. Facing the mirror with a hand mirror angled behind him, Wyatt made long careful swipes until he was left with a bald dome and tightly trimmed hair above his ears and at the back of his head. He looked thinner, sharper, like a man who lived a life of the mind. Finally he put on a pair of prescription glasses. He hadn't needed glasses, according to the one-hour dispensing optician, and so the lens adjustment was mild, but what the optician hadn't known was that Wyatt didn't want anyone to wonder why he had plain glass in his lenses and that Wyatt's real purpose in getting glasses was the heavy black frame. It altered his face completely.

It was a one-hour drive to Devonport. The ferry's departure time was 6 P.M., but the company asked passengers to be on board well before that, and the hire car had to be returned, so Wyatt left Flowerdale at three o'clock in the afternoon. He wore light cotton trousers, a polo shirt, and a lined woollen windproof jacket. He looked like a teacher or a priest in civvies. The heavy glasses transformed the cast of his face, from prohibition and wariness to internal musing and melancholy.

At five o'clock Wyatt found himself being swept by a crowd of people past drink machines, video games, slot machines and knots of smokers around barrelly chrome ashtrays, into corridors that led to the staircase at the midpoint of the ship. It linked all of the floors, and he plunged down to D deck. Here the air rushed in the vents, and he bumped shoulders with passengers who had nowhere better to go. His cabin when he got to it was like a tomb, pinkish grey, as disagreeable as the holiday flat in Devonport. He went in carefully, checking corners, checking the shadows. Wyatt lived in corners and shadows and that's where the end would come for him.

He ate upstairs, at a table next to a window, only the black night and the waves outside the salt-scummed glass. Inside the glass it was a world of scratchy muzak, kids erupting through doors, overweight men and women, smoke, and the mulish, quickly combustible emotions of the herd.

He slept badly. The ferry shuddered through the night. The next morning he made his way to the dining room but, realizing that he was to be penned like a sheep again and expected to eat like a pig at a trough, he grabbed an apple and a banana and made his way out onto the upper deck, where the wind was cold and clean and empty.

When the public-address system crackled into life, asking drivers to go to their cars, Wyatt went below, retrieved his overnight bag, and waited at the lifts. He chose an elderly couple. They were tottering toward the lifts, fighting a clutter of string bags and cases and each other.

"May I help you?"

"Help the wife throw some of this junk overboard," the man said.

"Charlie, shut up," the woman said. She smiled at Wyatt. "That would be most kind."

The man looked Wyatt up and down. "You going to your car?"

Wyatt laughed. "I don't drive. I'm on foot. I just thought you might need a hand." He reached for a case. "These look heavy."

He saw that he'd disarmed them. The woman gave up a case and a shoulder bag to him, the man a second shoulder bag.

"Most kind of you."

They stepped out of the lift into a claustrophobic iron shelf, the air full of fumes and echoes, the cars lined up like capsules in a pillbox. The elderly couple's car was a small blue Golf.

"If you'd care to squeeze in with a couple of doddery old fools," the woman said, "we'd be pleased to drop you somewhere, wouldn't we, Charlie?"

"Of course."

Wyatt rubbed his bald patch, feigning embarrassment. "Oh, I'm sure you don't want to—"

"Don't be silly," the old woman said. "We live in Hawthorn. We could drop you right in the center of the city."

"In that case," Wyatt said, "I'd be glad to take you up on your kind offer."

By 8:30 they were leaving the dockland. Wyatt felt safe. He wouldn't have felt so safe on foot, eyes watching him file off the ferry.

Wyatt didn't know what sort of hours his nephew kept. Besides, he wanted to approach Raymond with better information than the boy had provided at Hastings a week ago. Wyatt waved goodbye to the elderly couple on Bourke Street and caught a taxi to the University of Technology in West Heidelberg.

Twenty minutes later he was walking through to a broad lawn at the center of the campus. According to the map displayed at the main gate, the R.J.L. Hawke School of Burmese Studies was the building facing the lawn from the west. He found a bench near a pond and stretched in the sun. There were few students about, fewer staff. The university had once merely called itself an institute of technology, and it appeared that the word "technology" had determined the creative hand of the architects, for the place was universally ugly and pragmatic. No imaginative spark could ever be nourished in its stolid buildings. They dated from the 1960s and squatted among untidy eucalypts like grey bunkers. Here and there an external wall was pebble-dashed or set with glazed pink and grey tiles in outdated attempts at a stylistic flourish, but the general effect was depressing. No one ran or whistled or walked with a bounce or conferred earnestly with a friend. Wyatt imagined the humorless lectures and tutorials, the staff down at the mouth because of budget cuts and job uncertainty and the ever-present jibe: "It's not a real university. It's just a tech."

He eyed the School of Burmese Studies. It had a look of temporary flashness, an effect encouraged by a new roof and plenty of smoky glass. Workmen were still renovating the interior; Wyatt could see them coming and going with electrical flex, plasterboard, tins of paint, and ladders from a makeshift depot behind a cyclone security fence adjacent to the side entrance. Power to the building itself had been turned off. The workmen were relying on an external cable from the mains, looped like a thick black snake to a wooden pole staked temporarily in the lawn outside the security fence.

Chaos and clutter. He liked that. He looked more closely at the building. There were half a dozen trades represented by the workmen. Along with everyday tools they surrounded themselves with specialist equipment, supplies, and vehicles. In one corner of the makeshift depot was a stack of plasterboard under a tarpaulin. In another was a portable tin shed. Through the open door Wyatt could see buckets of paint. The air-conditioning subcontractor had claimed a third corner, his lengths of galvanized conduits, angle bends, grilles, and ducts scattered as though to help the earth exhale. There were ladders, copper and PVC tubing, reels of flex. In the fourth corner was a rubbish skip, overflowing with broken plasterboard, strips of wood, glass, aluminium window frames, tubes and hosing, and empty paint tins. Vans and small trucks and utilities came and went through the morning. They bore stains and rust and crumpled panels, and they leaked unburnt exhaust gases into the atmosphere. Some of these vehicles would be locked in overnight, Wyatt guessed.

He began to formulate questions and answers. At midday he strolled through to a cafeteria, bought a sandwich, and prowled the perimeter of the university, mentally mapping the configuration of roads and buildings. The campus wore a kind of down-at-heel, blue-collar innocence. It wasn't geared to anticipating holdups, burglaries, or heists of any kind, only pilfering from the union building shops and theft from the library.

By two o'clock Wyatt was on a different bench at a different point of the main lawn. He watched, read a newspaper, sometimes ambled across to the men's in the library basement. The newspaper carried an update on Steer's break from prison. He'd first caught the story from a discarded *Mercury* on the ferry. Since then a man matching Steer's description had disappeared near a roadblock in the Western District. Wyatt had no thoughts on the matter of Steer other than that, no matter where Steer went to ground, he'd be difficult to find. He'd once trained with Steer, and could attest to the man's gifts.

Chapter 22

Ninety minutes after breaking Steer from the remand prison, they had been back at the house in Warrandyte. The drive in darkness across from the Hume Freeway had been hell for Raymond. He had nothing in common with the Meickle woman, and all she could talk about was Steer, carrying on about how she'd given up everything for him, would walk through fire and water, so what was going on? Why had he cleared out like that? Where was he going? When would he be back? Would he be back? On and on.

They had left the car at the rear of the little house and gone inside. There she had clutched Raymond's arm. "Ray? He will be back, won't he?"

Raymond shook her off. "How the hell would I know? I'm going to bed."

Wait with Denise until I get back, that had been Steer's instruction. One thing was for sure, Raymond was earning his money on this particular job.

The next day had been hell, rained all day, and now a new

day was dawning, hell all the way, cooped up together, no topic in common except Steer. The Meickle woman was all pink and damp from two days of bawling her eyes out. She looked like some small, hairless albino dog, Raymond thought.

"I gave up my career for him," she said.

Raymond flicked through his *Jaguar Car Club* magazine. He didn't know why he'd joined. Okay if you wanted to wear a tweed sports coat and go on a fun run through the Dandenong Ranges, stop in a picnic spot, and have your picture taken for the magazine. Okay if you wanted to be buttonholed by some little twerp from the social committee. Okay if you wanted to read a blow-by-blow description in jokey prose about changing the diff oil in a '68 S-type.

He yawned massively. The sun was pouring through the glass wall at the rear of the house. He'd slept well, had toast and coffee, and here it was, only nine in the morning. The long hours lay ahead like a sentence. Couldn't even call anyone on the phone; it had been cut off while the owners were away. Raymond had the patience to stake out a country bank for a day or more, no problem, but he didn't know if he could just sit around like this for much longer. Casing a bank was different. There you had something to aim for, to look forward to. Here it was all up in the air.

"We could be waiting for nothing," Denise said. "He just used me."

Raymond stood, prowled the perimeter of the little room, looked out upon the forest with his fists crammed into the back pockets of his Levis. "Look, he's probably got some dough stashed away somewhere. Gone to get it."

Denise Meickle shook her head emphatically behind him. He saw it like a moon reflected in the glass. "Chaffey takes care of Tony's money matters."

That was interesting. Raymond turned. "Chaffey is Steer's banker?"

"It's safer that way."

"Huh."

Raymond sank into an armchair, hunted in the cane magazine rack for something better to read. He turned to the back of the *New Idea*, looked at the candid shots of the rich and famous. Fergie's tits, Richard Gere shopping incognito, Australia's own Nicole Kidman on a beach with her sister and a heap of kids.

Still only 9:30. "Want another coffee, Denise?"

"I mean, how long do we wait? When do we know there's no point in waiting for him?"

"Got me there, Denise."

He found the Maxwell House and spooned coffee and sugar into a mug. Turned on the kettle, then discovered it was switched off at the wall. Lunch. At least there was that to look forward to. He peered in the refrigerator. They had to shop. Get him out of the house at least.

Denise had trailed after him into the kitchen. She climbed onto a stool at the bench. "Or what if he's had an accident? What then? He'll be arrested. If he's hurt, he'll need me, he'll call for me. I'll have to come, even if it means I'll be arrested as well."

"Are you mad? There's no fucking way that *I'm* going to gaol for your boyfriend."

Raymond slammed the cutlery drawer. Jesus Christ, what a stupid bitch. "We need some things at the shop," he said finally.

"I'll stay here," Denise said complacently. "He may come back."

Raymond hadn't intended to take her with him in the first place. "Anything you need in particular?"

"A paper," she said. She gave a coy little shiver. "I want to see if they spelt my name right. They could even have pictures."

Raymond went cold. Pictures. He forced himself to relax. Sure, they'd have pictures of Steer and Denise; no reason why they'd have a picture of him.

"And orange juice and vodka," she said.

Good. Drink yourself into a stupor. "Got any cash?"

Denise turned sourly and went to her room. She came back, carelessly shoved a folded fifty at him, as if offering a tip to an undeserving waiter. "I want change."

"You're a sweetheart, Denise. I'd go for you myself if you weren't already taken."

The reply strangled in her throat and the tears spilled. She turned away from him and Raymond shrugged and left the house.

In a shopping center over the next ridge he bought a *Herald Sun*, groceries, and vodka. Steer and Denise were on page three. The photo of Denise was ten years out of date. Her aunt in Cranbourne begged her to notify the police that she was still alive. There was no one who wanted Steer back. Raymond found himself referred to simply as "the getaway driver."

He sat in the Jag and used the car phone. Got the answering machine at Vallance's flat in Hastings; no Vallance or Roden registered at the Windsor. Raymond felt frustration begin to settle in his bones. If Allie had been around he could have slipped down to the city this afternoon, fucked her brains out for a couple of hours, been back in time to babysit Denise before it got dark. He looked at his watch. Only another eight hours of daylight to get through.

Raymond drove back to the house, Allie stirring in his mind's eye. There would be time, if he could find her. He had until midnight before he was supposed to take Steer to meet the coastal freighter—that's if Steer showed up. Raymond had his doubts. Steer was probably well away by now. He'd done a runner, had his own agenda, wanted to dump old Denise without having to listen to a lot of crap first.

At one o'clock Denise said, two vodkas under her belt, "Where are you going?"

"Out," Raymond said.

"Where? Tony might come."

"Face it Denise, he's long gone."

Her face dissolved again. "Don't say that. Wait with me, please?"

He unhooked her stumpy fingers from his sleeve. "I'll be back early evening, okay? I can't hang around here all day. Got things to do. Got a life of my own, you know."

"You've been paid to look after me."

Raymond pointed at the vodka bottle. "Suck more piss. Dull the pain."

He left her crumpling behind him and whisked the Jag down into the city. Called at his flat, slipped on his good gear, went to the casino, feeling as eager as a kid at school who had the hots for someone.

But Allie wasn't there. Nor was Vallance.

And so he sat at his table and, in a cold rage, gambled away a third of the fifteen thousand dollar fee that Chaffey had given him to spring Steer from gaol, leaving him short for the deposit he'd promised Vallance.

The Warrandyte house was in darkness when he got back. Raymond's mood by now was *fuck this for a joke*, and he went in with Denise's shopping list Ruger in his hand, jacking a round into the chamber, screwing on the suppressor.

The place stank, as if she'd been drinking all day, shut away in misery, too depressed to turn the lights on when the sun went down.

Unless the cops had been. Unless Steer had some little surprise lined up for him.

Raymond edged through the dark house, letting the bitter disappointments of his afternoon give way to hair-trigger nerve and preparedness. He heard the floorboards, saw the shape poised against the moonlit window, and raised the Ruger to fire.

But it was Denise, foggy with booze. She slurred her lover's name. "Tony?"

Raymond scraped his hand over the wall, looking for the light switch. He couldn't find it, so let his eyes adjust to the tricky light of the moon filtering through the crowding trees outside the house. "No such luck."

She came across the room, only half comprehending him. "Ray? You brought Tony with you?"

"Face it, Denise, he's done a runner."

She wailed. Raymond had never heard anyone wail before. It acted on him like a migraine, like fingernails screeching down a blackboard, and he put both hands to his head to make it go away. The Ruger knocked his skull. "Ouch. Will you fucking quit that?"

She stopped a meter away, her mouth wide, tears glistening on her face. "He's hurt somewhere, I just know it."

"Get your act together, Denise."

She made to turn away. "I should ring the hospitals."

Raymond yanked her around by the arm. "Yeah, right, ring the cops as well while you're at it."

She stood miserably then gathered herself and said, with drunken cunning, "You've got a phone in your car."

"Forget it."

She came chest to chest with him. "Just a couple of calls. I won't give our names. Please? Pretty please?"

Revulsion welled in Raymond. He pushed her hands away. "You disgust me."

She changed again, fierce and concentrated now, intent on prising the Ruger away from him. "You can't talk to me like that."

They seemed to perform a kind of shuffling dance across the

floorboards. At one point the suppressor on the barrel of the Ruger flipped up and smacked bruisingly against Raymond's cheek. "Christ, will you bloody well—"

He should have switched the gun to safety when he had the chance. He should have shoved it away in his waistband. It went *phut* in the tangle of their hands and Denise's head snapped back. Her fingers clenched, relaxed, and she dropped to the carpet like a stone.

He found the light switch and with the return of his senses, Raymond saw that Denise had been shot smack bang in the center of her face. His first reaction was to swallow, once, again. He opened his mouth to speak. He shivered, looked around for help.

A moment later he shook off his attack of nerves. *Serves the bitch right*, he thought. She was redundant anyway.

The more he thought about it, the more he realized that what they didn't know wouldn't hurt them—Chaffey, Steer, the police. Yeah, she'd simply decided she couldn't hack the pressure any longer and shot through, caught the first bus to Queensland.

He wondered if he was losing his edge a little. He'd always felt in control before. Allie Roden, the treasure—they were doing something to him.

The jitters came when he wiped the place clean, buried Denise with her stuff, and drove back to his flat. The jitters threatened to shake him apart when, as he turned the key in his front door, a hand clamped on his arm and a voice growled, "Raymond."

Chapter 23

"Take it easy, son," Wyatt said. "Didn't mean to scare you."

Raymond breathed out heavily. "You're a sight for sore eyes. Come in."

They walked through to the kitchen, where Wyatt peered keenly at his nephew under the unremitting fluorescent light. "Are you okay?"

There was a bruise on Raymond's face. He wore a distracted air, an edge of hysteria under it. He gathered himself. "I'm fine. Rough night, that's all."

"Six o'clock in the morning. A long night."

"Yeah, well, you know," Raymond said.

"There's blood on your sleeve."

Wyatt saw his nephew start violently, turn his shirtsleeve this way and that. "This guy tried to mug me."

"Where?"

Raymond blinked, grew more concentrated. "King Street,

outside one of the clubs. I fought the bastard off. Anyhow, what about you? What gives with the haircut?"

Wyatt rubbed his shaven dome. "I'm a known face in this city."

Raymond shrugged, losing interest. Then he yawned widely and stretched his back. "Rough night."

Wyatt said, "I want you to take a shower, then have something to eat, then we'll talk."

"I'm all right."

"No you're not."

Raymond weaved out of the room. The shower, food and coffee gave him the sharp edge that Wyatt was looking for. Half an hour later they sat at a table in the harsh kitchen light, Wyatt with a pad and a pen at his elbow.

"Right. I went to look at the building where the paintings are stored. It can be done." He drew rapidly. "These are possible exits. As you can see, the place is like a sieve."

Raymond gulped a second cup of coffee. "Chaffey mentioned nightwatchmen."

"I'd rather deal with a nightwatchman than cameras and alarms," Wyatt said.

"What do we do if it goes wrong?"

Wyatt looked at him. "Let's say you walk into one of your bush banks to rob it. There's a cop at the counter, paying his mortgage. What do you do?"

Raymond shrugged. "Turn around and walk away from it."

"Exactly."

There was a pause.

"What's on your mind, Ray?"

"Just going through the scenarios. We could shoot through, not bother with Chaffey. I mean, fifty grand each, it's not much. We'd get more selling the collection ourselves. Or," he said, grinning, "I could shoot through on you, take the collection with me."

Wyatt didn't take the joke. "I'd hunt you down. Never cheat your partners. They have very long memories. When it's an institution, there's nothing personal at stake. With a partner there is, and if he's like me, he'll hunt you down."

Raymond shrugged. He was full of sulky gestures, like a teenager out to stir an adult. "Why not invest the paintings in some coke, some pink rock from Thailand? Cut it, sell it, we'd get a million back easy, maybe more."

Wyatt seemed to snap like a coiled spring. His expression was direct and unnerving as he grabbed Raymond by the throat. "No drugs."

"Lighten up, Unc. Just a joke."

"I never deal with that stuff."

"Maybe you should go with the flow. You're out of date."

Wyatt knew that his nephew was stirring. Even so, a rare feeling welled up in him. He wanted to slap some sense into his nephew. If Raymond were anyone else he'd have walked away.

But he said nothing, just let the heat dissipate.

Raymond felt the force of Wyatt's stare. He said uneasily, "It's okay. I was only joking. I'm not a user or anything."

"Good."

After another pause, Raymond asked, genuinely wanting to know: "How come you don't pull the big jobs any more? You loaded or something, just keeping your hand in for the fun of it? These paintings, for fifty grand, hardly your style."

The answer rose unbidden in Wyatt. "I'm tired."

Raymond stared at him, his brow creasing. He seemed to be touched a little with panic and confusion, as though Wyatt had identified a hard, necessary, and inescapable fact of existence. "You? No way known."

Wyatt said, "All right. Not tired. But there are two things going against me: technology and time. It's getting harder to break into places, and the people I used to trust are all dead and gone."

As if to bolster Wyatt's spirits, Raymond clapped his hands together and said, "I won't let you down."

"Good. Time to let this Chaffey character know."

Raymond stared at the wall, grimaced as if swamped by bad thoughts. "Chaffey?"

"It's his job," Wyatt said, frowning. "Don't you want to see him?"

Raymond said vaguely, "She's jake, no worries."

Raymond phoned, and Wyatt noticed that he leapt right in, choking Chaffey off, only letting him suggest somewhere to meet.

It was the grounds of Montsalvat, the artist's colony in Eltham. Chaffey had a ticket to an afternoon jazz concert, and met them on a grassy slope above the hall. It was a good place for a meeting, Wyatt thought, but Raymond's mood had changed again as they'd driven deeper into the hills, a reversal to his nervy distracted state, as if the trees and folds and gullies were populated by demons.

But all that mattered was the job, and Chaffey. Wyatt assessed the big man, noting the unhealthy skin, his wheezing chest and damp neck and brow, then looked for what the face and eyes might reveal, some predisposition that told Wyatt he should walk away from this.

He was startled to find that Chaffey was returning the intense scrutiny. "Heard you were at the center of a ruckus in the city the other day."

Wyatt waited a beat, then said, "The police know it was me?"

"Yes."

"That's all they know?"

"Yes."

"How did you hear about it?"

"Pal," the big man said, "I'm a lawyer. I hear things."

"I'm here," Wyatt said. "They're no closer to finding me."

"Glad to hear it," Chaffey said. He moved decisively, placing a briefcase on the grass between them, patting it. "Take this when you leave here. It contains a list of the works my client wants, their dimensions, and floor plans of the building."

"Your client wants only some of the paintings?"

"A big Whiteley, two Tuckers, two Booths, three Lloyd Rees drawings, a Dobell and four Heysen watercolors."

"You say you've got floor plans. I hope they can't be traced back to you."

Chaffey shook his head. "I applied for them in the name of the firm renovating the building."

"Who's your client?"

Chaffey laughed. "The wife of the man who put the collection together. According to her, the paintings were a present, but the husband pissed off overseas with his secretary, owing a few million to his creditors, so the collection was sold off and the wife got nothing. She's understandably upset, wants her paintings back."

"What makes you think the cops won't look closely at her?"

"They will, but she's no longer around. The paintings are going straight to New York, where she lives now. You deliver the paintings to me, you get paid, I crate them up and courier them to her, that's how it works."

Raymond stretched out in the sun. He'd shaken off his mood. "You're her lawyer?"

"No."

"How do you know her?"

"Our kids went to the same school."

If often happened that unimaginable lives were revealed to Wyatt. They were lives lived parallel to his, defined by money and respectability, private schools and skiing holidays, Volvo station wagons and horse-riding teenage daughters, divorces and charity functions. Now and then his life and theirs veered course sufficiently to intersect. Whose life was the most honest or the least unrealistic, he couldn't say.

He followed the exchange between Chaffey and his nephew. Raymond was asking all the right questions. "The same school? So there's no other connection between you? The cops won't come looking at you?"

"No."

"Good. Because I don't want to sit on these paintings while the air clears. I need my fifty grand the moment we hand you the pictures."

Chaffey said nothing while a woman wheeling a pram passed close behind them. When it was safe, he cocked his head. "Gambling debt, young Raymond?"

"Business deal," Raymond said, and Wyatt and Chaffey looked at him, waiting, but Raymond didn't elaborate.

"How about things in general?" Chaffey asked. "Everything going according to plan, Ray? No hiccups?"

There was something about this, some sort of private communication. Wyatt watched and listened, but all Raymond said was, "No dramas my end, Chafe, no worries."

"Glad to hear it," Chaffey said. He climbed in painful stages to his feet. "Keep me posted."

Wyatt shook his head. "We're dropping out of sight till this is over."

Chapter 24

Back at Raymond's flat, Wyatt felt himself switching gears, taking in his surroundings as he retreated mentally from matters of escape routes and the unknown. He had a few days up his sleeve for planning the job. Right now there was Raymond and Raymond's flat.

Wyatt didn't feel comfortable. Unless the apartment was being watched, he was safe enough staying there, but he hated not having control. Nothing here belonged to him, he liked to have his feet at ground level, not ten floors above the street, and he had to wear a public face.

Perhaps that's why he scribbled down his Tasmanian address for Raymond. "Treat it strictly as a way out if you're in trouble," he said. "Somewhere to go if you can't come back here."

Raymond held the slip of notepaper in both hands, examined it, made to slip it into his wallet. "Thanks."

Wyatt's fingers clamped on his wrist. "Memorise it," he said.

Raymond sighed raggedly. He looked bad to Wyatt, the

demons still chasing around in his head. Wyatt saw his nephew mouth the address silently, close his eyes in concentration, blink open again.

"Got it. Where the hell is Flowerdale?"

"Between Burnie and Stanley on the north coast."

"Yeah, right, lots of café society, nightclubs," Raymond said, screwing the paper scrap into a ball and tossing it into an ashtray. They both looked at it. "Suppose you want me to swallow it now?" he said sourly.

Wyatt said nothing, simply put a match to the paper and crossed to the window to stare down at the river and the city.

He liked to know that he was close to water. Water was alive. It meant contradictory things to him: stealth, power, restlessness, an endless calm.

He heard a groan and turned to see Raymond clutch himself, his face white. "My guts have been playing up."

"Food poisoning?"

"Maybe nerves," Raymond said, grinning weakly. "No, don't worry, nerves of steel."

"There's a chemist downstairs."

"Good idea."

Raymond left the flat. Wyatt stood for some time, staring at the river, seeing the job ahead of them. He became conscious of the open door to Ray's room, and wandered across to the door and went in. The boy was untidy. Wyatt knew that he employed a cleaning lady, so presumably there was no incentive for him to be neat.

The cash box sat in darkness on a high shelf, under an empty nylon overnight bag. The key was in it. It surprised Wyatt, seeing Steer there, gazing coldly at the camera. Raymond stood next to him, grinning. The photograph had been taken at night, near trees. He found Steer in another photograph, his arms around a short, broad-faced unhappy woman, the woman close to him as though she wanted to meld herself with him.

Wyatt hunted deeper into the cashbox. Newspaper clippings, going back several years. He recognized some of the headlines: AIRPORT BULLION HEIST was an old one, one of his own. More recently there were clippings about the bush bandit, highlighted here and there with strokes from a yellow pen.

And clippings about Steer's escape from gaol.

When Raymond returned to the flat, Wyatt forearmed him across the throat, propelling him backward and pinning him to the wall. He said, in a low, dangerous rasp: "I'm going to remove my arm now. I will ask you some questions. You will answer them."

Raymond's eyes were wide and aggrieved. He forced a nod.

Wyatt let him go. "Good. Did you help Steer escape?"

"Me?"

Wyatt's forearm went back across his nephew's windpipe. He relaxed it again.

Raymond gasped, "Yeah, it was me."

"The papers say the woman was involved."

"Her and me."

"Where is Steer now?"

Raymond swallowed. "Overseas. That was the deal. Boat from Lakes Entrance."

"The woman, too?"

"Her, too."

"Raymond, Steer was seen running from a roadblock recently."

"Well, yeah, then he turned up as planned where I was minding the girlfriend and I took both of them to the boat. I swear."

Wyatt stepped back. He took Raymond into the bedroom and

forced his head onto the cashbox, then off again, as if Raymond were a dog who'd fouled the carpet. "This is what an amateur does. He keeps all his little mementos with him, letters from his pals, photos, clippings, stuff that will tie him to everything he's ever done or come near. It's stupid, stupid. It'll get you gaol time. It's sentimental and there's no room for sentiment in this game. Burn this crap."

"Fuck you—"

In a cold rage, Wyatt gathered the spill and took it into the bathroom. He made a bonfire of it in the bath, and when it was reduced to ashes he sluiced it all away with the shower nozzle, his own long career and his nephew's shorter one.

He went out to Raymond. "Your life starts over again," he said, as if the past had had nothing to do with anything.

"You bastard."

"Ray, you're on your own now. I'm out of this. You're on your own."

Wyatt said it heatedly, a new sensation for him, almost as if he hadn't decided on the words but let them pop out.

Raymond grew passionate in the face of them. "Haven't I always been alone? You dumped me and my mum. You dumped your family. I thought I'd at least see you when she died, but you couldn't give a stuff, couldn't even come to the funeral."

Wyatt had been on the run when it happened. He'd heard the news weeks later. Seeing the fretfulness, frustration, and sore feelings in his nephew now, he allowed his expression to soften. It was intended to be a look of compassion, but Wyatt was not good at compassion and something—his habitual scepticism, his permanently unimpressed view of the world—made itself known to Raymond. Raymond swung away and left the room.

Wyatt followed him. "Tell me about the break-out."

Raymond said, "You still here? I thought you were pissing off on me again."

Wyatt said, "I was too hasty. I apologise. But I don't like surprises. Did Chaffey put the escape together?"

Raymond nodded.

"You did it for a fee?"

"Yes."

"What do you know about Steer?"

Wyatt saw his nephew shrug. "What's there to know? Chaffey's his lawyer."

"You don't know anything of Steer's history? Chaffey didn't tell you anything about that?"

"No. Why should he? What's Steer to you?"

"An old grievance, that's all," Wyatt said. Steer was a loose end, like a live power line snaking around on the ground nearby, but one that could be attended to later. He made for his room and packed his bag.

"So, this is it?" Raymond said.

"The job's still on. But we both need to find somewhere else to stay. Separate places."

"You must be joking."

"I never joke."

"You ought to try it sometime," Raymond said.

Chapter 25

From the driver's seat of her car, Liz Redding watched Raymond
Wyatt stride down the slope toward her, into the underground
residents' garage. The location was a pricey motel in Parkville,
and Raymond was whistling, swinging a key ring around his index
finger. He passed right by her. Two days earlier she'd followed him
here from his apartment block on the other side of the city, but
this was her first close look at him. A more sullen version of his
uncle's hooked face and hooded eyes. The same black hair, only
worn longer, so long that it hung greasily about his face, meaning
he was forever clawing it back with his left hand. The hands: not
shapely and nimble. Shorter, thicker. And while Raymond was
built like Wyatt—tall, sinuous, compact, with a quickness under
the still surface—he lacked strength and vigor. Liz Redding
formed an impression of unfocused courage and grand, frustrated
ambitions.

His Jaguar was in the far corner. Liz started her car and
ploughed up the ramp and onto the street, where she slowed down,

as though looking for an address, one eye on the rearview mirror. She wanted to be moving when the Jaguar appeared behind her. If Raymond saw a parked car turn on its lights and pull in behind him, he'd know he was being tailed and he'd try to lose her. Of course he might turn left out of the driveway, in which case she'd switch off her headlights, U-turn, and follow him for a distance before switching on again, but she doubted that he would turn left. Twice now she'd followed him right, down to Gatehouse Street, then around by the cemetery to north Carlton, before losing him.

She inched along, whistling impatiently. A moment later, headlights rose and dipped behind her as the Jaguar entered the street. The car accelerated, coming up behind her, and Liz turned on her indicator and steered into the kerb, letting him pass. She saw his brake lights flare at the corner. He turned right, then was gone from sight. Liz pulled out again and put her foot down.

She relaxed when she was on the Parade, settling in three car lengths behind the Jaguar. Even if he veered onto an unfamiliar route or tried to be evasive, she was reasonably confident of staying with him. The XJ6 was a distinctive car, but even so, earlier in the day she'd detailed the rear of the big car with small strips of reflective tape. They were under the bumper and not immediately apparent to someone standing close to the car, but clearly visible to anyone farther back in a car at night, showing as an irregular red pattern in the headlights. Raymond's car was unmistakeable. He could merge with a freeway of similar cars and Liz would know him.

The minutes passed. Raymond followed the cemetery around and headed toward Princes Street. Now and then he altered speed or skipped lanes, as though to shake off a tail, but Liz didn't let herself be drawn. He was simply going through the motions. He probably imagined a tail even when he went out for bread and milk. She stayed where she was, in the left lane, at the speed limit, more or less.

Liz followed the XJ6 to Alexander Parade and onto the Doncaster Freeway. Raymond wasn't so tricky now. He kept to one lane and to the speed limit, a young blade tooling along in his glossy big car. Liz drifted close to him from time to time and had a clear view through the rear window of the casual way he draped himself in the car, one shoulder against the door, one hand on the wheel, the other along the top of the passenger seat.

Raymond took the Bourke Road exit, winding through the cuttings in the little hills of Ivanhoe and down into West Heidelberg. He surprised her by parking in a side street and strolling into the grounds of the University of Technology. Liz parked, got out, removed the reflective tape from the XJ6, and hurried after him, into a world of lighted footpaths between clumps of shrubbery and a hotchpotch of blockish buildings, many of them well lit. Even so, the place seemed dark and creepy, and she thought of the female students braving the shadows at night, on their way to a lecture or back to their cars in the vast lots.

Raymond came to a bench seat near a pond. Here there was plenty of light, even a couple of smooching students on the grass, and then, for the first time in two weeks, she saw Wyatt. He wore a dark cap and a dark zippered jacket and was standing rock still, watching from the corner of a nearby building. She knew that look: dark, sceptical, wary as a cat. He didn't spot her. He began to approach his nephew, moving with an easy fluid lope that could have turned into an attack or flight in an eyeblink. Part of her stirred, transforming the loose grace of his walk into the more concentrated grace of his hands and his body as he'd touched and flowed with her on their narrow bunk aboard the yacht. Despite the distance, she noted tight lines of exhaustion, even of sadness, on Wyatt's face. She was reminded of a prowling creature aware of its needs and the hunter's weaknesses.

What broke the spell for her was Wyatt lifting his cap to scratch his head. He'd shaved off most of his hair. He looked monkish, like a grim recluse in an old painting.

Liz watched them for an hour. They could pass as mature-aged students, she realized, taking a break from the library stacks. One of them went for takeaway coffee from a machine. They talked, strolled, sat again. Once when a nightwatchman went by she saw a subtle stiffening of their spines, and after a while it occurred to her that Wyatt and his nephew were watching a particular building. She would have to find out why. It had a shut-down look about it, a cyclone security fence around an area of building supplies against one wall.

She wondered what Vallance had to do with it. Twice she'd seen Vallance and a young woman arrive at Raymond's flat. She'd also seen the woman visit Raymond alone, at the motel in Parkville. Liz had had dealings with Vallance before and couldn't see someone like Wyatt getting involved with him. Maybe Raymond had his own agenda. It might be worth tipping the wink to her friends in CIB. They could pull Vallance and the woman. If nothing else, it might scare Raymond and Wyatt into walking away from this job, whatever it was. She hated to think of Wyatt in gaol. She'd crossed a line and was walking with him now.

Wyatt parted from his nephew at nine, when the late lectures and tutorials broke. Liz knew where Raymond lived. Time to learn where Wyatt had his bolthole.

Chapter 26

"Okay, Raymond," Vallance said, "just so you know I haven't been twiddling my thumbs."

For this meeting, Raymond was back in his apartment. Fuck Wyatt. He watched as Vallance cleared a space on the coffee table and stacked it with brochures and photocopied price lists. "I can get this stuff in Geelong, Williamstown, Devonport, Port Melbourne."

He spread the documents over the table and tapped with a bony finger. "This here's your up-market scuba gear and tanks. Tough, good air capacity. Okay, this is an underwater scooter."

The brochure showed a clumsy machine trailing a diver. Raymond leaned over the table for a better look. Allie was next to him on the couch. That was good, heat from her long thigh.

"I know it looks like a handful of buckets and tubes welded together," Vallance said, "but you can cover a lot of ground quickly. Plus it's fitted with a metal detector. A scooter's good for backing up a visual search in clearish water less than fifteen meters, which part of our area is."

Vallance slid another brochure across the table. "This here's your proton magnetometer."

Raymond saw a diver in murky water, holding the center point of a transverse bar to which two sensor heads, shaped like small torpedoes, had been fitted. "How does it work?"

"See this cable? It connects with a monitor in the boat. The boat tows you in a predetermined search pattern over the seabed. The sensors pick up anything made of iron or steel, like cannon or anchors, even if they're a hundred and fifty meters under. One of these babies will pick up a large steel ship up to a quarter of a mile away."

Raymond leaned forward and indicated a different brochure. "What about this? Looks like a vacuum cleaner."

"Good one," Vallance said. "That's more or less what it is and how it works. Depending on where you come from it's called a dredger or an airlift. Operated by a compressor on the surface. We'll have a lot of sand and sediment to clear away."

Where Vallance couldn't see it, Allie was scratching her bare toes against Raymond's ankle again. He returned the pressure. "Pretty impressive."

Vallance nodded. "So you can see how it all mounts up. Equipment, plus a boat with plenty of deck and hold area, doesn't take long to eat up a quarter of a million bucks in this game."

Raymond was fascinated by the machines. "What's this?"

He indicated a photograph of a diver dwarfed by two massive hollow tubes, suspended on either side of him at the rear of a ship.

"It's a prop wash," Vallance said. "You anchor your salvage vessel thoroughly fore and aft, so she doesn't move, place these tubes over each propeller, then run the motors. The wash effect gets directed downward, like a whirlpool, and it blows away the bottom sediment. Clears a large area *molto* quickly. Not much good in water over fifteen meters, but I thought we should get one, given that we can't afford to hang around the wreck for too long."

Raymond said, "But if it's just lying there, like the stuff we saw the other day, why all the bother?"

"It's not just lying there. If you took the trouble you might pick up twenty or thirty grand's worth of gold coins just wearing scuba gear, but the bulk of it will be intact, buried deep somewhere."

Raymond nodded. "So all this equipment's available now?"

"It is."

"None of it's cheap?"

"Not if it's top grade." Vallance numbered his fingers. "You've got your hiring fee, insurance, transport costs, incidentals like our accommodation and ferry charges. I won't lie to you, it's going to cost. But consider the return. Jesus Christ, unimaginable."

Raymond felt more alive than he'd ever been. Part of him wondered if his judgement was shot, but mostly he itched for Allie Roden, itched for the treasure. "Need a big boat for all this stuff."

"That's right."

"So have you got one lined up?"

"Down in Geelong," Vallance said. "Look, Raymond, I won't bullshit you, we have to move fast on this. Most of the syndicate's money is already accounted for. Plus, one guy pulled out at the last minute, putting more pressure on us. I'll need at least a deposit from you, as soon as possible. I mean, no offense, but I'll have to look elsewhere for funding if you decide you can't—"

"I can pay."

"Sorry, put it another way—if you don't wish to get involved."

"You said someone pulled out?"

Allie spoke for the first time, rolling her eyes in exasperation at what fate had delivered. "We were *this close* to finalizing the deal, and he pulled the plug. Now we have to start again, put out feelers, make approaches . . ."

"So there's nothing to stop me from buying *two* syndicate shares?" Raymond asked.

She looked at him doubtfully, mouth open, thinking about it. "No reason why not," she said slowly. "What do you think, Brian?"

Vallance was sharper. "When I see some hard cash, Ray, then we can discuss whether or not you buy one share, two shares, or none at all."

Raymond swallowed. Denise Meickle swam into his thoughts again, her unappealing face, her slack body flipping into the hole he'd dug for her. He tried to shrug her away. He was a few days away from fifty grand. Hundred grand, if he had Wyatt's share. Fucking Wyatt, big man with a reputation, sneaks a look at his private things and puts a match to his memories. What did Wyatt want with fifty grand, anyway, considering he had the jewels and God knows what else stashed away in his house across Bass Strait. Wyatt, a bully and a coward, just like his brother, Raymond's father.

"You'll get your money," Raymond said.

There was another scenario—pay Vallance with a million bucks' worth of paintings.

Vallance was staring at him disbelievingly, but then smiled and folded away the brochures. "I know you will. I have every faith."

"Not all my assets are liquid at the moment," Raymond said. "Like, a lot of it's tied up in art."

Vallance peered doubtfully at Raymond's walls: a Formula 1 racing car, a Ken Done print.

"Not this crap," Raymond said. "The real thing, stored in a vault. Family heirlooms." He named the artists Chaffey had listed.

Vallance looked interested. "Dinkum?"

"My Dobell," Raymond said, "could fucking *buy* you a boat, let alone rent it."

"Well," Vallance said, climbing to his feet, "I'm certainly interested, but, like I said, I need cash." He looked at his watch. "Be back in a couple of hours. There's some other people I want to show these brochures to."

Allie showed him to the door, kissed him on his leathery cheek, closed the door, and leaned her long back against it, smiling languidly at Raymond. "Two hours."

She uncoiled from the door. She loped across the carpet on her bare feet and pulled his head to hers, periodically laughing with pleasure, a dark laugh deep in her throat. They undressed. She breathed, "What would you like me to do?" and Raymond stroked her, feeling her moist heat. "Wash me with your cunt," he said, and heard the laugh again, her sheer delight in him. He gave himself up to the sensations, a kind of floating. She was good for him. She had the power to drive Denise Meickle from his head.

At the end of it she propped herself on her elbow and moodily traced his ribcage. "I wish I could see you all the time, instead of snatching an hour here and there."

"Me, too."

She laughed shyly. "For the first time in a long while I've been thinking more than one week ahead, you know?"

"Do I figure into your plans?"

She said simply, "Yes."

"Dump old Brian?"

She sighed. "It's run its course anyway."

"He won't like it."

She shrugged. "So? It happens all the time."

"Make sure you dump him *after* he pays me," Raymond said.

She looked at him. He tried to fathom it. "Or dump him permanently at the site, if you know what I mean."

Raymond found himself saying, "You know the paintings I said I owned?"

"Yes."

Raymond told her about the university, the R.J.L. Hawke School of Burmese Studies. He told her about Wyatt and the bush bandit and the prison break, not bragging, just wanting her to know.

Awe and excitement settled on her face. "Is *that* who you are?" she said.

Chapter 27

"Why a van?" Raymond wanted to know. "Why not something fast?"

"We're going to attract attention if we walk out with a heap of paintings and try to stuff them into the boot of your Jag. Not that they'd fit in the boot."

"So concealment is the issue."

"Yes."

They were sitting across from the R.J.L. Hawke building again, ham sandwiches and cans of mineral water between them on the grass, talking it through. Seagulls wanted their crusts. Students sauntered past, the women with books clasped to their chests, the men with no books at all.

Raymond concentrated, biting his lower lip. "You know when you stole that Picasso?"

Wyatt nodded.

"The word is you hid in the building overnight, walked out with it the next day."

"Yes."

In 1986 a bent art dealer from Prahran had hired Wyatt to steal *Weeping Woman* from the National Gallery on St. Kilda Road. His story was that a rich man with a grudge was putting up the money. The painting was bound for Europe. Wyatt had got the painting out, concealed as a folio purchased from the Gallery's bookshop, but the job had gone sour after that and the painting had found its way back to the gallery.

"We could do the same," Raymond said.

Wyatt wanted his nephew to think it through. "But in this case we'll have fifteen paintings on our hands, some the size of the top of a kitchen table. For that we need a van, whether we stay on the premises overnight or not."

Raymond mused glumly for a while. "Is there anything to say the paintings have to stay in their frames?"

"You're on the right track."

"We roll them up in something."

"Yes."

"Plumbers, electricians, they carry stuff around in long PVC cylinders."

"You're getting there," Wyatt said.

Raymond flung a crust to the gulls. "How come we have to go through this rigmarole? If you already know what you want, how come you don't just tell me and I'll do it."

"I'm not telling you anything. You're arriving at the answers yourself."

"Am I a kid? Is this school? Arsehole."

Wyatt looked away. He was learning how young Raymond was, after all. He wanted, by asking questions, to encourage thought. He wanted Raymond to identify problems and offer solutions, to inquire and speculate. In Wyatt's game, working well was at once thinking well, perceiving well, and acting well.

And he couldn't deny that Raymond had badly unsettled him. That box of photographs, letters, and clippings—amateurish and oddly human and ordinary. It was an aspect of human nature that Wyatt could not understand. But the boy's most damaging bombshell concerned Steer. Steer was a problem, and, because he'd helped Steer to escape, so was Raymond. Wyatt wondered if, even now, as he sat watching workmen come in and out of the target building, the police had a firm idea who was behind Steer's escape. When this job was over, he'd cut all ties with the boy.

He watched the ducks among the reeds, watched the students, watched a pigeon settle on the temporary power cable at the building site. "Okay, when would you do it?"

"Overnight Saturday."

"Why?"

"Not many people around."

"And?"

"The robbery wouldn't be discovered till the Monday morning."

"True. Though we could also go in on Friday night."

"I wouldn't."

"Why not?"

Raymond indicated the workmen. "Those blokes will be working there the next morning."

Wyatt nodded. "On the other hand, there won't be any students or staff around on Saturday, not when they'd have to endure drills and hammers and transistor radios all day, and that means there'd be no one to spot that the paintings were gone. The workmen are unlikely to notice or care one way or the other."

"So there's no reason for anyone to go into the library storeroom until Monday."

"Exactly."

"What it boils down to is how do we get them out, and when?"

Raymond shrugged. "At least we don't have to think about alarms and cameras."

"But we do have to think about nightwatchmen."

"Concealment," Raymond muttered. "Conceal the paintings in the PVC cylinders, conceal who we are."

"Yes."

They fell into silence. Eventually Raymond said, "We need to look like we belong."

"Clearly."

Silence.

"Cleaning staff?" Raymond suggested.

Wyatt shook his head. "Not in a building that's still being renovated."

Irritation came quickly over Wyatt's nephew. "Chaffey should have thought of all this."

Wyatt sensed that the irritation owed itself more to the palpable sense of competition and resentment that had developed between them than to Chaffey's lack of solid information. He said nothing. If he put things right for the people he dealt with, then he'd never get any work done, that's how he saw it.

Besides, Raymond had to learn: the job came first. He had to curb his impulses. Wyatt tried to look back along the years. Had he ever been impatient? Had he ever been young? It sometimes seemed to him that he'd landed on the earth fully formed and always this age, always this careful. If there had been a time when he was a child, a youth, it was according to the calendar, not character. He supposed it was a shame.

Now he did say something. "Ray, ultimately it's up to us."

But Raymond wasn't listening. His eyes were narrow and sharp. "When I was at school we had an asbestos scare."

"Asbestos?"

"These blokes came and looked in the ceilings. Nothing

happened, the place was clean, but it scared the shit out of everyone."

"Go on."

Raymond rubbed his hands together, thinking. "Right. Let's say we pose as electricians. We run the risk of meeting the real ones. If we go in as asbestos inspectors, not only will we be alone in that, we'll look as if we belong and everyone will avoid us."

Wyatt turned, gave a snatched smile. It was his way of praising Raymond, but Raymond misread it.

"So? You do better."

"It's good, Ray."

The heat subsided in Raymond. He turned away, muttering, "Let's go get that van."

Chapter 28

Raymond took them to a multi-level car park in Chadstone. They had the number plates, from a wrecked Volkswagen gathering dust outside a crash repairers in Altona—now all they needed was the vehicle.

"Check that panel van," Raymond said, some time later.

A white Falcon, with a roof rack and windows in the rear compartment. It wasn't a commercial vehicle, but could be adapted without much trouble. They tailed it to the upper level and watched the driver, an elderly man, park, lock up, and shuffle across to the lift.

When the man was gone, Raymond approached the driver's door with a tire iron. He levered a gap between the door frame and the pillar, then slid a loop of stiff plastic binding tape behind the glass. Wyatt looked intently both ways along the sloping ramp. Wednesday, early afternoon. They needed to be on the campus grounds by four on Friday, giving them two days in which to alter the van.

He turned back, just as Raymond caught the latch with the plastic hook and pulled upward. There was a click. "You little beauty."

Raymond slipped behind the wheel. Wyatt had stiffened, expecting an alarm, but there was silence. Raymond broke it. Suddenly all elbows and clenched teeth, he wrenched at the ignition with the tire iron, splintering the plastic casing and laying bare the electronics behind it. He fired up the motor, grinning at Wyatt from amidst the wreckage. "Piece of cake."

"And obvious to anyone who takes a gander through the window," Wyatt said. "Wait there."

He went to the front of the van and then to the rear, hooking the stolen plates over the originals. He ran his hand inside the rear wheel arch. The box was small, metal, with a sliding lid and a magnetized base. The elderly man's spare house and van keys nestled inside the box and Wyatt dropped them in his nephew's lap as he slid into the passenger seat. He said nothing, just buckled his seat belt, but his silence was hard and cold.

Raymond stared at the keys. There was always a smile close to the surface and it broke out over his sulky face now. "Ahh," he scoffed, "more fun this way."

That afternoon they repaired the ignition lock and took the panel van to be resprayed green at a place in Richmond—$999 of Wyatt's dwindling reserves. On Thursday they stencilled the sides of the van with the words "Asbestos Removal Services," and filled the rear compartment with empty boxes, a stepladder and several lengths of PVC tubing.

They went in on Friday afternoon at four o'clock. They wore overalls and Wyatt carried a clipboard and an aluminium document case. They parked the van inside the enclosure as though they belonged to the place, got out, and asked around for the foreman.

"That's me."

He was a large, loosely built man with a face mapped by broken capillaries. Friday, four o'clock. Wyatt was betting that all the man wanted to do was knock off and head for the pub.

"EPA sent us," he said, flashing his clipboard.

The foreman was looking in alarm at the van. "Didn't know we was working around asbestos. Bastards didn't tell us that."

"You may not be. This is routine, that's all."

"I mean, fuck, you been inside the place? Blokes have been breathing dust for days."

"There's dust and there's dust," Wyatt said.

The foreman looked at his watch. "It's nearly knocking-off time. I'm out of here in ten minutes myself. Locking the gate and I'm gone."

"I understand."

"So you can't park your van here. I'm locking up."

"That's all right," Raymond said. "We'll leave it overnight, catch a bus home."

"His wife," Wyatt explained. "She doesn't want the van parked out the front of the house. Nor does mine. Can't say I blame them."

The foreman licked dry lips. "Do what you like. It's no skin off my nose."

"The van's clean," Wyatt said. "No contamination. It's just the idea that gets to people."

"You can say that again."

Men began to stream from the work site. The foreman forgot about Wyatt and Raymond, and under the cover of men shouting, stripping off their overalls and cleaning brushes and rolling up flex, they loaded their arms with lengths of PVC tubing and entered the building.

According to the floor plans supplied by Chaffey, the

departmental library was on the first floor. They went up the stairs, whistling, ready to discuss the football if they encountered anyone, and found the first floor deserted and quiet, heavy with the smell of paint, plaster, and sealant. They drew on latex gloves and made their way into the gloom, Wyatt counting the doors.

"This one."

He tried the handle. It was locked. He took a set of picks from his overalls and leaned over the lock. Holding the tension pick at an angle, he teased with the raking pick, turning the tumblers. When it was done he breathed out, straightened and pushed open the door.

They went in, locking the door behind them. It was close and comfortable in the library. The carpet was thick, the shelves crammed with textbooks, folios, and theses. A few small desks, a table and chairs, a sofa. "Somewhere to sleep," Wyatt murmured.

"Together?"

"One sleeps, one keeps watch."

"Lighten up. I was only joking."

There was more light here than in the corridor. The outside wall was mostly glass and let in the lowering sun.

Wyatt crossed the room to a door set into the end wall, between two bookcases. He heard a rustle and scrape behind him and dropped to the floor.

"Quit that."

Raymond was in the act of closing the curtains. "We'll be seen."

"We'll be seen from outside drawing the curtains when this room should be empty," Wyatt said.

"Now we can't turn the lights on."

"The power's been disconnected, remember?"

Raymond flung himself onto a sofa. "You talk to me like I was a kid in school. Fucking well tell me what to do, then."

Wyatt felt complicated emotions for his nephew, composed of love, hate and frustration. But some of the fire had gone out of Raymond, leaving him edgy and cautious, and that was a good thing as far as Wyatt was concerned. Keeping his voice mild, he clicked open the aluminium case and said, "We work by natural light, there'll be a moon tonight, plus these." He indicated a pair of torches, their lenses all but taped over. "They give a narrow band. Just don't flash them toward the window."

Raymond shrugged. It was a shrug of tiredness, of a short, spluttering fuse. "One thing I've learned, I work better alone."

"Come on, son, help me with the storeroom lock."

"Son" was as close to love as Wyatt could get, but saw by the twist of his nephew's face that he'd chosen the wrong word.

Time for that later. He opened the storeroom door and they went in. "If you hold one of the torches, I'll start sorting."

The storeroom was small and windowless. Shelves started at waist height and were crammed with books, journals, binding boards, and gluepots. The paintings were under the bottom shelves, leaning against two of the walls.

"So far so good," Wyatt said.

experience with staking out and robbing banks, but Raymond's jiggling foot and pacing betrayed him.

Tiring of Raymond creaking out of an armchair for another prowl of the little library, he hissed, "It's nine hours until morning. Get some sleep."

Raymond dropped to the carpet and stretched out. He sighed, he rolled onto his back and made shapes with his fingers against the moonlight. "How come you've never been caught? Pure fluke?"

It irritated Wyatt to hear his life boiled down to notions of luck and chance. "I've made mistakes. Things happened that shouldn't have happened, but because I hadn't thought through everything, not because my luck was bad. And if the cops didn't nab me then it wasn't because my luck was good—I made sure they didn't nab me."

"You shot to kill."

Wyatt hated this. "I go into a job knowing that the gun in my pocket is going to add ten years to the sentence if I get caught, but also knowing it's there to save my life, not take someone else's."

Wyatt saw a shadow, a kind of inward look or memory or emotional trace, pass across his nephew's face. He pursued it. "Have you used a gun? Do you want to?"

Raymond shook his head violently. "No, no. Just saw someone get shot once, that's all."

"Not a pretty sight?"

Raymond wouldn't look at his uncle. "No."

Wyatt let the silence mount. Then he went on. "Let's say you get stopped by a cop or a guard tomorrow morning. Weigh up the situation. If you can shut him up just by talking to him, do it. Tap him on the head if necessary, but not so hard you'll cause a brain injury. Better to render him unconscious by cutting off his air, one hand over the mouth, the other squeezing the throat. He'll thrash around, but that uses up energy and sooner or later he'll be out

Chapter 29

Wyatt began to sort through the paintings, choosing those on Chaffey's shopping list. He saw that he was effectively gutting the collection. At least half of the works were worthless, minor drawings and prints. The collection's value lay in the big name oils and watercolors.

Darkness fell over the city. They cleared an area of carpet in the library and began to painstakingly remove each painting from its frame. Wyatt knew that it was necessary, but hated doing it. Each canvas, taut and humming, became lifeless the moment the tension was gone from it. Rolling it into a cylinder and sliding it into a PVC tube was a final barbarity. But it happened. It was what art thieves did. *I can't afford to get sentimental over a few paintings*, Wyatt told himself. It hadn't always been like that for him. He'd once burnt a painting rather than let possession of it earn him a gaol sentence.

The long night was ahead of them. Wyatt was used to the waiting game and he'd supposed his nephew would be, given his cold. Anything in preference to shooting or seriously hurting someone."

"You've shot people."

"I've shot people who have crossed me or threatened to kill me or left me no other choice. Never a panic shooting, never a thrill shooting, never a shooting because I had a sore head that day and was easily irritated, never a shooting because it was the easy way out."

Raymond draped an arm over his eyes.

Wyatt watched his nephew. "You're feeling the pressure. So am I. It's normal. I'd be worried if you weren't."

"What if it looks wrong when we go out the door in the morning?"

"Then drop everything, walk away, hang the time and effort and expense. In fact, I always expect the worst. That way I won't be surprised or caught off guard."

"They could have plainclothes out there in the morning, seeing where the paintings are going to."

Wyatt shrugged. "Check for what's not obvious. Look at body language, the way someone's holding himself or walking. The way he's dressed. If everyone else is in shirtsleeves but one man is wearing a jacket, maybe he's also wearing a concealed gun."

Raymond laughed harshly. "Aim at a cop, hit a uni student."

"You could try running at the cop."

"*At* him?"

"It will rattle his nerves, stop him aiming properly."

Raymond still lay stretched out on the carpet. He crossed his feet at the ankles and laced his fingers behind his head. "I'll be glad when we're in the van. Downhill all the way after that."

"There's a big difference between getting away and staying away. There's burning our clothes so we can't be tied to the scene, all those carpet fibres collecting on your back, for example. There's wiping down and dumping the van. There's the changeover with Chaffey. A long way to go."

"Sometimes, Uncle Wyatt, you're a sanctimonious fucking pain in the neck."

Wyatt felt obscurely hurt. He said nothing.

"I mean," Raymond said, "don't you ever *enjoy* what you're doing?"

To his own surprise, the words spilled out of Wyatt: "Ray, if you've got the nerve and the ability, there's nothing like it on earth. I know I said drop a job if there's the slightest doubt, but I also know there's something addictive about testing the odds, being your own boss, making enough from one strike that would take a nine-to-fiver ten years to amass. But the money's not it, not even ten percent of it." He paused, searching for the words he wanted, then said, "I like using my head and body well, doing what comes naturally to me in a risky game."

There was silence. Then Raymond whistled ironically, raised one fist like a winning athlete, said *"Fucking A!"*

The wrong tone to use with Wyatt. Wyatt turned away, wondering what he was doing here, with this kid. Raymond was a distraction. When Wyatt worked with another man he didn't want to have him always at the back of his mind, having to think of his safety, wondering if he'd do his side of the job properly.

A dull flash in the corner of his eye. Raymond was sitting with his back to a filing cabinet now, spinning a coin. It caught the moonlight as it rose from his thumb, reached an apex, fell into his palm again. It seemed clear to Wyatt that he was expected to notice the coin. He said, "Where did you get that?"

Raymond lifted his chin defiantly. "My mate Vallance. He's a diver, found this wreck. Been there a hundred and seventy years."

He went on to explain about the *Eliza Dean*. When he was finished, Wyatt reached out a hand. "May I?"

He caught the coin. He recognized it as a Spanish dollar. There had been one in a coin collection he'd once stolen from a house in Toorak.

"This is quite valuable."

"Vallance reckons a hundred and seventy-five dollars. And there's more where it came from."

Wyatt let the silence gather around them. "Are you and Vallance mounting a salvage operation? Is that why you need the money so badly, the business matter you mentioned the other day?"

"So what if I am?"

"How do you know it's not a rip-off?"

Raymond flared, "Give me some credit. I'm not naïve. I dived on the wreck myself, saw the coins there with my own eyes. Plus, this is a proper syndicate."

"If you say so."

"Fuck you. I tell you what, keep the fucking coin. I won't need it."

The boy was a bundle of nerves. Wyatt pocketed the silver dollar—for the time being, to keep him happy—and said gently, "It's late. Get some sleep. I'll wake you at two, you wake me again at six."

And so they passed the long night. At six o'clock on Saturday morning they shared a flask of coffee and a couple of fruit pies. At 7:30 the first workmen arrived. By mid morning the R.J.L. Hawke building rang to hammers, jigsaws, whistled tunes, and radios tuned to weekend sports talkback programs.

Wyatt and Raymond slipped out of the library just before ten o'clock. They walked along the corridor, down the stairs, and out to the panel van with the PVC cylinders under their arms. Some of the workmen were outside the building, smoking, yarning, tipping the dregs of their morning tea onto the ground. They saw Wyatt and Raymond and went quiet and still.

"Morning," Wyatt said. He read their hostility. It was all focused on that word "asbestos." With any luck, he thought, after a weekend of football replays and the pub and squabbling kids, asbestos will be all they remember.

The foreman scowled. "Didn't see you arrive. You blokes find anything?"

"Clean as a whistle," Wyatt said, and felt them relax around him.

Wyatt and his nephew loaded the stolen paintings into the rear of the panel van and drove slowly through the university grounds and out onto the depressed streets of West Heidelberg. Wyatt turned on the radio, fiddled with it, found the ten o'clock news.

The first item was the discovery of the body of Steer's girlfriend, Denise Meickle, in a shallow grave in Warrandyte. She had been shot in the head.

Chapter 30

Wyatt yanked hard on the wheel, bringing the panel van in a skewing slide across the path of an oncoming bus and onto the forecourt of an abandoned Mobil station. He steered down the side of the service bay and braked nose to nose with a wheelless Cortina.

"You useless little shit."

He turned, looked at his nephew. The movement was slow and deliberate, his expression carrying a chill. He took in one aspect of Raymond after another, quartering him, finally resting on Raymond's face. "You shot her."

"No way. Probably Steer, not me."

Wyatt sidearmed his nephew in the throat, a chop with the side of his hand that rocked Raymond's head like a punching bag.

Raymond screamed once, a choked, liquid cry of pain and fear, his eyes wild. "Don't hit me. Just don't hit me. All my life I've been hit."

For just an instant, Wyatt stood apart from himself and didn't like the man he saw there, sitting cold and clenched, ready to strike out again. He wished that Raymond were a stranger to him. He was linked to Raymond by blood, and that was the complicating factor. He put his arm down, relaxed his fist. "I won't hit you, but I want you to tell me about it."

Raymond croaked, "It wasn't me killed the bitch. Steer."

Wyatt aimed for Raymond's stomach this time, a hard jab that drove the breath from his body. "You were in a mess when I found you outside the door of your flat. A rough night out, you said, but there was blood on your sleeve and you looked bad. You shot her and it made you sick to the stomach."

There was a tearing sob. "She wouldn't shut up. Always snivelling on about Steer, had he run out on her, would she see him again, what should she do—it drove me nuts. I had to get out. When I came back the place was dark and I shot her by accident. Hey, what are you doing?"

Wyatt removed the keys from the ignition. The story sounded more or less right. But even if Raymond hadn't shot Steer's girlfriend, the complication was more than Wyatt was prepared to stand. He cranked down his window and tossed the keys over the dividing fence into an overgrown garden.

"What the fuck?"

Wyatt reached for his door handle. "We abandon. We walk away from this like it never happened."

Hysteria crept into Raymond's voice. He clutched Wyatt's arm. "We can't abandon. We got out safely, we got the paintings. There's no need."

"It all feels wrong now. Instinct tells me to get out. You shot her—you've probably still got the gun in your possession—and that means double the heat. How do I know what other ways you've fucked up? Maybe you were seen shopping in Warrandyte. Maybe she was found a few days ago and all this time they've been moving against you. We're walking away from this, Ray. You go your way, I'll go mine. That's it."

As Wyatt reached for the door, Raymond tugged the Ruger automatic from an inside pocket of his overalls. He ground the muzzle against the hinge of Wyatt's jaw, hissed: "We take the paintings to Chaffey, now. We get our money. Then we split."

"Too dangerous."

"I need that money."

"Walk away from it Ray," Wyatt said, reaching up idly to push the gun away, then leaning under the dash and ripping hard on the wiring.

Sobbing, "You bastard," Raymond smacked the butt of the Ruger down on Wyatt's bare scalp, full force, several times. Wyatt felt a disabling blackness. Raymond's sobs receded behind a foggy wall of pain, blood pooled in the hollow of his collarbone, and all he wanted to do was curl up and nurse the pain. He had no inclination for fighting or flight.

Much later, Wyatt awoke, an island of misery behind the steering wheel of a stolen panel van. He shivered. He could not control his teeth, feverish and unquiet in his mouth. He remembered Liz Redding's warm hands on his poor skull. They had been two days out of Vanuatu when a rogue wave knocked him off his feet and he clipped his forehead on the mast. Sometimes she came back to him like that.

When he felt strong enough to move, he eased onto the ground and around to the rear doors of the van. He looked in. One of the PVC cylinders was missing. Wyatt supposed that that made sense, if you were Raymond. The cylinders were long and awkward. You'd be able to carry one on foot on a suburban street, not four. And you would take one; you wouldn't leave it and save your skin.

There was a water tap against the back wall of the service

station. Wyatt washed away the blood, stripped off his overalls, put the cap over his injured skull and walked to the nearest set of traffic lights. A cruising cab picked him up. He gave the address of his motel in Preston.

Some procedures were automatic for Wyatt. He paid off the driver two blocks from the motel, then walked past the place a couple of times, on the opposite side of the street. Finally he crossed to the motel and followed the path around the car park to his room. He stood for a while, watching. He wondered if they'd be waiting for him.

At that moment a cleaner appeared around the corner, pushing a cart crammed with brooms, buckets, and plastic bottles. A small transistor radio swung by its strap on the chrome handle. Wyatt changed direction until he was a meter away from her and murmured, "I'm checking out of fourteen. The room's clear, if you want to start there."

She peered doubtfully at the first door in the row. He saw that she liked routine. You started at the end and worked your way along. But the first door and two others wore "Don't Disturb" signs, so the pattern was broken anyway. "No skin off my nose."

"Thanks."

Wyatt walked away. He stationed himself behind a potted ornamental tree near the pump shed of the motel's swimming pool and watched the cleaner. She inserted the key in the lock, swung open the door to his room, pushed the cart in. Nothing. No surprises or shouts or backpedalling feet.

It took her ten minutes, and when she was done and in the next room, Wyatt went in. He moved carefully, stationing a chair under the bathroom ceiling fan, climbing onto it in stages, and taking his time to unscrew the fan. No sudden movements. He had a few hundred dollars there, a new set of papers.

Wyatt put an end to his hard, unravelling morning with a

shower. He should have run, but just then he was too bone-weary, too dazed, too swamped by scalding, comforting water to care.

He towelled himself dry at the window, looking out onto the courtyard, keeping his movements slow, containing the pain. He blinked away the water from his eyelashes. It was Liz Redding, standing perfectly still and contemplative in the weird green light of the swimming pool awning, watching his room, watching his shape in the window. When he blinked again, she'd turned away, and the last he saw of her was the long slope of her back and the tilt of her hips as she bent to fit a key into the lock of a small white Corolla.

But it was the wrong key. She straightened to examine the others on the keyring. Wyatt thought there was time. This didn't have to be the last that he saw of her.

Chapter 31

Raymond's hand was sticky. He looked down: blood gouts, from when he'd smacked Wyatt in the head with the butt of his Ruger. Shifting casually, leaning forward and down as if to scratch his leg, he wiped his fingers on his sock, hoping the driver hadn't noticed the blood or the concealment. He straightened again, looked over into the back seat. Red palm prints on the PVC cylinder. Raymond drew in a ragged breath, whistled to calm his nerves.

They stopped at a light. The cab driver punched a thick finger at the keys of his dispatch screen, cursing softly. "Hate this fucking thing."

Raymond grunted.

A message came up. The driver peered at it. "Call Mr. Atkins at Thomastown Legal Aid? Christ in hell, what's she done now?"

Raymond figured that the cab driver was not so likely to remember him or smeared blood if he had troubles of his own. "What's the problem?"

The driver glanced in the rearview mirror. He was late for the green light and had been tooted from behind. "Up yours, arsehole," he said, giving the finger to the other driver. The cab streaked away across the intersection. "The daughter," he explained. "She wags school, goes shoplifting with a gang." Both hands lifted from the wheel, slammed down again in a gesture of hopelessness. "I mean, what can you do? They don't teach them anything at school any more. You try to do the right thing at home, teach them what's right and wrong, and some pinko prick from the teachers' college undoes it all or they get in with some gang and skip school. I blame the drugs myself. The economy. Who cares about the family, these days? It's dog eat dog out there."

Raymond wanted to say, "Back up a step, you've lost me," but mention of family and school gangs and shoplifting reminded him of his own high school years, reminded him of Wyatt, of Wyatt not being around for him. He wet the index finger of his left hand, rubbed where Wyatt's blood clung stubbornly to the palm and wrist of his right hand. He couldn't understand why he hadn't popped the bastard. Pow, center of the fucking head.

Raymond didn't want to think that he wasn't up to it a second time.

"What's in the tube?"

Raymond stiffened. "What?"

The driver jerked his head toward the back seat. "You got plans there? You know, blueprints?"

Raymond coughed. "Got it in one."

"What, you a builder?"

"Work for one," Raymond said.

Inside he was screaming, *Come on, come on, get me home.*

Where he'd shower, put on good clean daks, phone Chaffey with the news that Wyatt had fucked up.

"You wouldn't like to run an eye over my place? House needs restumping, salt damp coming up the chimney, thinking of putting in one of them pergolas out the back."

Raymond squeezed his eyes shut. His head ached. He saw the endless blighted suburbs, populated by blokes like this driver, their wives and kids, from cradle to grave worried about money. That wasn't *his* career path, no way known. He opened his eyes. "Sorry. We specialise in shithouses for government schools."

"Fair enough," the cab driver said. "Just thought I'd ask, you never know."

They lapsed into silence. Raymond watched the city skyline fill the windscreen as they trundled along Nicholson and down into streets that saw little of the sun. On the other side of the city the driver said, "You'll have to guide me. Southbank's changing that quickly, I can't keep up."

Raymond paid him off outside the ABC studios, then cut through a side street to his apartment building.

Upstairs he sponged away the blood from the cylinder then stood for ten minutes in a lacerating stream of hot water in his bathroom. It occurred to him then that he was stupid, coming back to the flat. He threw on some clothes, packed a bag and took the stairwell down to the car park beneath the building.

When he was on the move again, well clear of the concrete bunker, aiming the Jag for the southeastern freeway, he dialled Chaffey on his car phone.

"Chafe? Guess who?" he said, when Chaffey answered.

Chaffey was quick. He didn't use Raymond's name. "Why are you calling?"

"We have a problem."

A pause. "Our mutual friend?"

Raymond's brow furrowed. "Pardon?"

"Your work colleague," said Chaffey heavily.

"Oh, right, I'm with you now," Raymond said. "He's . . . got a sore head."

The agitation was clear in Chaffey's voice. "Permanent?"

"Wish it was," Raymond said.

Chaffey left that alone. "So the deal fell through?"

Raymond tried to think how to put this. "We got about a third of what we budgeted for."

"A third? All or nothing, that was the understanding. Otherwise the contract is null and void."

Raymond swallowed. Just lately he'd been subject to panic attacks, swamping out of nowhere, making his heart race, his mouth go dry. He related the attacks to his obsession with the treasure, his anxiety about missing out. The attacks had been worse since the shooting in Warrandyte. He said to Chaffey, trying to control the hysteria in his voice:

"Chafe, I successfully completed part of the job and I deserve part payment. Not my fault our mutual friend dipped out."

"You say he dipped out, he decided it was a no goer?"

Raymond barrelled the big car along the Hoddle Street overpass. Football traffic choked Hoddle Street and the inbound lanes of the freeway. "That's what I'm saying. Blame him it went wrong, not me."

Chaffey was clipped and certain. "One, he must have had a good reason. Two, a third of the goods is no good to me. No payment. Nothing. Zero. Three, I've been trying to contact you all week. The goods from that other deal failed to arrive in New Zealand. I'd like to know why." He paused. "There's a knock on the door. Call me in a couple of days."

The line went dead.

That didn't stop Raymond. He drove on, thinking about the cash in Chaffey's house: his lawyer's fortune, the payment for the paintings, the money he kept stashed there for the crooks he represented. Chaffey and Wyatt were probably similar in that way, never spent on the here and now, always had a stash hidden away somewhere.

Chapter 32

"I liked you better when you had a head of hair."

"It'll grow back."

Her fingers explored his scalp. "Nasty gash he gave you."

Wyatt swayed a little, let her change the dressing. It was the next morning and he felt clean and calm. He was fully dressed, but hadn't spent the night fully dressed. Nor had Liz Redding. There hadn't been an erotic charge in their shared nakedness through the night, only comfort and an essential, restorative warmth. He closed his eyes and leaned against her. In a sense he was surrendering. The emotion was alien, oddly welcome. He'd lived a life built upon vigilance and sharp edges. It would be good to let go once in a while.

Liz smoothed a strip of sterile tape over the cleaned gash on his head and sat back to look at him, her hands in her lap. She looked fine and flashing to Wyatt—in good humor and ready to do combat with the world, using her head and her hands. He said, "Anything on the news?"

"Some kids were caught looting the van. The police are trying to track down where the paintings came from."

"They'll know soon enough. All you have to do is pick up that phone."

"I told you, I've been suspended. They're going to chuck the book at me. I don't care. I've had enough. Anyway, I'm a woman. There's nowhere for me to go. The boys have got the force sewn up."

Wyatt grunted. "Do yourself a favor then. Impress them. Bring me in."

"You came to me, remember."

Wyatt remembered. He had seen it as a private communication, a warning perhaps, Liz standing outside his motel like that. He could have slipped away. Instead, he'd stepped outside and crossed the car park and tapped her on the shoulder. She'd taken him to a different motel. Said she expected to be arrested if she went home.

There was the soft beat of her body next to him. He wasn't interested in her career, only her impulses. "Once a cop, always a cop," he said, more harshly than he'd intended.

She said miserably, the words springing from nowhere, "I love you."

Wyatt breathed in. Then he breathed out.

"What I mean is, you're in my thoughts all the time. I don't want anything to happen to you." She shrugged. "If that's what love is."

Wyatt looked around the room. It held no answers for him.

"I suppose," she said, "you want to run from me now that's out in the open?"

Wyatt thought of the unwanted clutter in his life and he thought about the absence of love in it. It was not an ordinary life. He liked it streamlined, but right now it was loaded with complications: Raymond, Chaffey, the dead woman in Warrandyte, Liz Redding, the paintings. As for love, that was another complication. Was it better than none at all? Meanwhile he could settle for an expression of it. He felt cold and ill. He picked her hands out of her lap, chafed them, placed them over his shoulders. "Make me warm again."

He saw that he'd put a foot wrong. A subtle change passed across Liz's face, as though a deep-seated pain were reasserting itself, drawing out her features, thinning and contracting her face in a kind of recoil. She pulled away from him and sat straight-backed, her chin lifted.

"Didn't you hear what I said? All this is momentous for me. You, my job. But everything with you is one way. I haven't a clue what you want or think."

Wyatt tried haltingly to discover, from speech, what it was he thought and felt and wanted. The effort exhausted him, bringing on a kind of electric blackness. His head buzzed and dizziness racked him briefly, and pain. When he came out of it he felt her hands on his cheeks. "You okay? You're very pale."

"Please, I feel cold."

She took him to the bed, removed his clothes, then her own, and the warmth revived him. "Gently does it," she said, easing him into her.

Later she curled up with him, murmured for a while, breathing against his neck, then fell heavily asleep. She was slack, heavy, peaceful, and close against him. Wyatt drew his arm out by degrees, swung his legs to the floor and stood. The room swayed and tilted. He closed his eyes, sat, and when the room righted itself, dressed carefully. His shoes presented a problem. He stood above them, clasped the back of a chair, wound his toes in, forced the heel down. The laces could wait; he needed to keep his head up.

The keys to her car were in a leather shoulder bag. He found a purse, a small box of tissues, tampons, moisturizing cream, and a mobile phone. Wyatt pocketed the keys, two hundred dollars, and the phone. He glanced at the bed. She was sleeping. He closed the door quietly behind him and pressed the gadget on the key ring to disengage the locks on her car.

They sprang open with a strangled electronic yelp, the driver's door creaked when he opened it, and Liz Redding, wrapped in a motel blanket, was at his window before he could start the car and drive away.

He sighed, wound down the window, and heard her fury and disappointment. "You bastard. Not again, I don't believe it."

Wyatt showed no embarrassment, no anger, no haste—only deliberation. "Liz, you belong here."

She stood away from him, suddenly exhausted, looking cold and vulnerable and insubstantial beneath the blanket. "I'm tired of this, Wyatt."

The pause was awkward. Wyatt thought: *I've constructed a life out of moving on.* It was easy. All you had to do was turn your back and put one foot after the other down the road. Would she stop him or wish him luck? It came down to disappointment. He'd disappointed her. But she was not vindictive. Wyatt suddenly felt obscurely grubby for trying to sneak away. His head boomed, a spike of pain behind his eyes. He leaned back and closed his eyes.

"You're not fit enough yet."

"You could be right," he said.

Some of Liz Redding's combativeness came back to her. "I want you."

"We're different."

"No we're not. I've got the Asahi jewels."

He opened his eyes. "Where?"

She jerked her head. "In my case. I went back to the yacht and found them. I intend to keep them, Wyatt. I intend to melt down the settings and sell the stones."

"They're fakes."

She laughed. "Is that what Heneker told you? I knew he smelt wrong. He was playing it both ways. If you get arrested, his firm gets the Asahi Collection back. If you don't, and he can deal with you again, he'd pay you some minimal reward for the so-called fakes and pocket the rest." She paused. "Wyatt, join me."

In the gathering silence they were both stubborn, waiting for a way out. Wyatt thought: *How calculated are her moves? Does she resemble me, or have the things I've done, the evasions, made her wary?* When doubts set in, you fix on what is known. Wyatt knew himself, he didn't know her. But he was beginning to, and that hadn't happened to him for a long time. He said, attempting a grin, "We can't stay here."

Chapter 33

The drive to Belgrave took fifty minutes, but when Raymond got there he found that Chaffey's house was shut up tight, curtains drawn, no car, no sign of life. He searched under flowerpots and mossy garden stones, but found no spare key. The door was deadlocked; there were bars over the windows and security company stickers on the glass. Surely Chaffey wouldn't have panicked and done a runner because the job went sour?

After that he tried Chaffey's office. The whole building was shut. Saturday.

Raymond felt spooked. He drove to Hastings with a sensation of guns at his back and dogs at his heels, expecting to be pinned to the ground by lights and clubs, but he completed the journey intact.

He wondered how he was going to play it with Vallance. Hold out for more time? Offer the paintings as collatoral? Offer to come on board as an employee? Holding out for more time seemed to be the best bet. He knew he couldn't get hard cash for the paintings in the PVC cylinder for weeks, maybe months.

Then again, he did have access to money. Wyatt would have heavy cash put away somewhere, maybe under the floorboards of his place in Tasmania. Plus he had things to settle with Wyatt, the old festering sore and now this more recent cunt act: the whole collection is in their hands and Wyatt walks out on the job as if the risks and rewards and hard work meant nothing at all.

In a slow pass along the street front outside Vallance's flat, Raymond noticed that the venetian blinds were closed and the front step was piled with newspapers. He felt the beginnings of another panic attack. Vallance had found other investors. Right now he was out diving on the wreck, stripping it bare. Leaving the Jag two blocks away, Raymond returned on foot and knocked on Vallance's door.

When there was no answer, he stepped back and examined the neighboring flats. They looked as mute and unlived in as Vallance's, and there was only a seagull watching him, so he lifted his foot and kicked at the lock until the flimsy wood splintered and he could push through into the stale interior.

Within a few minutes it occurred to him how temporary the flat was. A few days earlier, when he'd stayed the night here, his mind had been on his prick and the gold coin, so he hadn't noticed the bareness. Now the flat looked like what it was: a dingy place, probably rented furnished for a short term, the kind of place you walked away from.

Yet there were clothes in the closet and toiletries in the bathroom. Some eggs in the fridge. The answering machine was turned on.

Raymond thought his way into Vallance's skin. He'd fear burglars, a high unemployment place like this. Burglars headed for your usual places: cupboards, drawers, coat pockets, freezer compartment, under the lid of the cistern. Where wouldn't they look? Raymond started with the exhaust fans, one in the kitchen, the other in the bathroom. Nothing. But he kicked a tile on the bath and it clattered to the floor. Behind it were gold sovereigns, silver florins and gold and silver ingots, and it all fitted nicely into a red vinyl Thomas Cook bag.

The next step was Quincy. Raymond found the captain listed in the local phone book, a weatherboard house near the waterfront. Again parking the Jag some distance away, he returned on foot to scout around outside the back fence. It appeared to him that Quincy was out. His only impression was of silence and dashed hopes.

He vaulted the fence. A patch of buckled asphalt outside the back door told him something about Quincy's past couple of days. Empty gin and beer bottles, leaking their dregs into a cardboard box; a lumpish garbage bag slumped against the wall, ribbed and jointed within by tins, cigarette packets, chicken bones.

He had a clear view through the window to a greasy sink and an overflowing ashtray on the table. At the end of the kitchen was an archway, and beyond that, in the curtained gloom of the living area, Raymond saw the body of the sea captain.

He tried the rear door. It wasn't locked. He went through to Quincy expecting to encounter the odor of death, but only alcohol fumes and cigarette smoke thickened the air, and Quincy stirred when he prodded him.

"Where's Vallance and his bird?"

Quincy propped himself on an elbow, looked at Raymond, collapsed again. "Gone out for smokes, what do you reckon?"

Raymond opened the blinds and returned to Quincy, hauling roughly on his arms, pushing him into a chair, slapping his face left and right. "Are they out at the wreck? Are they stripping it?"

Quincy shook his head and pushed at Raymond's hands. "What do I know? They never told me nothing. They're all the fucking same, these city jokers."

Raymond wanted Quincy's intellect applied to this, not his feelings. He went into the kitchen and filled the electric kettle. A jar of instant coffee lay on its side in the cupboard above the sink. He spooned large quantities of coffee and sugar into a mug, added boiling water and milk, and made a weaker cup for himself.

He turned to find Quincy leaning in the archway, regarding him bleakly. "Just clear out, okay?"

He ignored him. "Drink this."

"Fuck off."

A memory boiled up in Raymond's head, of Denise Meickle and what he'd done about it. His vision went black for a few seconds. When it cleared he was still at the sink and Quincy was still alive, though pale and alarmed.

"Look, I don't know nothing," Quincy said, backing away. "The pair of them owe me six hundred flaming bucks, that's all I know."

"Have they been here in the past forty-eight hours?"

"Haven't seen them for days."

Raymond thought it over. "I want you to take me out to the wreck."

Quincy cocked his head. "It'll cost you."

Contempt and satisfaction clear on his face, Raymond slapped the red Thomas Cook bag into Quincy's hands and said, "Take a look in there."

Quincy peered in. He whistled.

"There's more where that lot came from," Raymond said. "Take me out, now, today, and you can have what's in the bag."

"It's a deal."

"Give me the bag," Raymond said. "You get to keep it later."

They walked out into the bright sun, where children rode bicycles and teenage boys tinkered with cars and women walked home from the supermarket. It was hot in the Jag. Raymond wound down his window, for cool air, for air that was not saturated with Quincy's pungent, boozy perspiration.

The marina was quiet under the wheeling sky. It seemed to Raymond that no one saw them prepare Quincy's rustbucket for the open sea, not until a voice heavy with authority said, "*Freeze.*"

Chapter 34

It had started with an anonymous phone call to CIB. The caller had been very specific, CIB had swooped outside the casino, and now it was paying off. As soon as Vallance and the girlfriend—and Christou, the poor sod they were putting the hard word on—arrived at the police complex, Gosse separated them and began by questioning Christou.

Then he went to Vallance and said, without preamble: "Mr. Christou said that you offered to show him a shipwreck site."

"Might have done. What's it to you? It's business, private, between me and him."

Gosse stared at Vallance. The man was a clothes horse: dark suit, expensive aftershave, a high gloss on his black shoes.

"He said that you were forming a syndicate and did he wish to invest."

"So? Nothing wrong with that."

"Is that where you find your suckers? The gaming tables?"

Gosse agreed with the Opposition that the casino was a blight on society. Certain crime statistics had skyrocketed because of it. Good people—including coppers—were blowing all they had on a throw of the dice or the fall of the cards. It made mugs of a lot of people, and attracted mugs, like this Christou character, who owned a cluster of market gardens and had more money than sense.

"Mr. Christou has given us a statement. In it he says that you showed him items of treasure from a wreck. Is that correct?"

Vallance's fingers went *tock, tock* on the interview table. He shrugged.

"Mr. Vallance, for the sake of the microphone, please answer yes or no."

"Yes."

"Coins, in fact. Are these the coins you showed him?"

Gosse poked a shoe-polish tin toward Vallance. The lid was off. There were two florins and a bronze token nestling in tissue paper. "Could be," Vallance said.

"No 'could be' about it. We found these in your possession. Now, where did you get them?"

"A shipwreck. Nothing wrong with that."

"I can think of several things wrong with it. For a start, you are obliged to inform the authorities. Have you done that?"

"Paperwork, bureaucrats," Vallance said. "All takes a while."

Gosse pressed on. "It's also a problem if the coins have been looted from a protected wreck. See what I mean?"

"It's not protected. I found it fair and square. It's not even on the register."

"So you don't mind if we have an expert look at these coins, Mr. Vallance?"

Vallance cracked a little. He wiped a bony finger across his upper lip. "Do what you like."

Gosse got up to leave the room, saying "Interview suspended" and the time for the tape, and pressing the pause button. As he got to the door, Vallance called out, "I asked for a lawyer. Where's my lawyer?"

"Legal Aid is stretched to the limit. There'll be a solicitor here to see you as soon as one's available."

Gosse stalked down the corridor. The sergeants' room was almost empty. A tired detective, rubbing his face, was yawning into the phone on his desk. Another detective was at the bank of filing cabinets.

"Where's Liz Redding?"

Both looked up. "Haven't seen her."

"I need her to look at some old coins. Tell her to contact me the minute she comes in."

Then Gosse went still, his eyes far away. "Get her on the blower."

"Sir?"

"Do it, ring her home number. *Now!*"

Shrugging, rolling his eyes at the other sergeant, the man at the desk referred to a list and punched in Liz Redding's number. They waited. The seconds mounted.

"Answering machine."

"She's done a runner," Gosse said. "I can feel it. Right. Find her. I want her brought in. Quick as you can."

"Right, sir."

Gosse was high in color now, the blood pounding in his head. "You," he said, pointing to the other sergeant. "Get hold of whoever we've got attached to that shipwreck protection outfit, get him or her over here at the double."

"Yes, boss."

Then Gosse gathered himself, counting slowly, and made his way to the interview room where Allie Roden was being held.

He stepped in quickly, pleasantly, a busy, efficient man with a job to do. He studied her file, letting the silence work on her, then looked up. "Well, you're in the poo, wouldn't you say?"

She was bored. "Would I?"

There were times when Gosse hated the games you had to play. They played their side of the game, you played yours. His head started to pound again. He decided to fight dirty. "We're filing a procurement charge. Mr. Christou said that he was being offered sex as an incentive to invest in a shipwreck syndicate."

She flared. "That's not true!"

"By far the more serious charge is theft from a shipwreck. According to Vallance, you have him in tow so that he can impress the mugs with his knowledge of diving and shipwreck history. It's your scheme, though, all the way, he says. You do all the heavy talking. And heavy breathing, if we're to believe Mr. Christou. And, frankly, I do."

"I don't know anything. I'm just along for the ride."

Gosse pushed his face close to hers. "Mr. Christou said that four investors were involved, fifty thousand each. Did you have sex with the other three? We'll find them soon enough. They have security videotapes at the casino. All we have to do is identify who you've been seen with."

She pouted. "Don't know anything."

She pronounced it *anythink*. The pout spoiled her looks. Her hair was dank and smelt of cigarettes, alcohol and expensive perfume soured by sweat. Breathing shallowly, Gosse sat back in his chair. He regarded her for some time, then went back along the corridor to Vallance.

"Miss Roden is quite upset. She says you made her have sex with these investors and one of them gave her herpes."

Vallance went white. His hands flashed to his groin. "That bitch."

"Is it true? Did you make her have sex with them?"

"There was only one guy interested in investing. Young bloke. Not Christou, whatever his name is."

Gosse said patiently, "Okay, only one prospective investor. I'll ask again, did you or did you not oblige Miss Roden to have sex with this investor so that he'd fork out fifty thousand dollars?"

Vallance snarled, "No. Look, I asked the bitch to be friendly, okay? Make the coffee, be around to answer questions, make hotel bookings, that type of thing. I certainly didn't ask her to sleep with this guy. Bloody hell, she's my bird. I'd like to throttle the bitch."

"You didn't know?"

"I had my suspicions." Vallance wriggled in his seat, as though his trousers were tight. "She could have taken better care, got him to wear a rubber at least."

"You're infected for life if it's herpes."

Vallance began to scratch and tug. "Fucking moll."

Gosse said, "Look at it this way. You'll do time, two, maybe three years, but the herpes will protect you from the hard men of the yard, keep them off you in the shower. You know, tell them you're infectious and they'll leave you alone. Of course, some of these guys have AIDS, so they won't care one way or the other."

"You lousy bastard."

"Make it easy on yourself. Get a load off your chest. Maybe the judge'll be lenient."

Vallance was staring at his hands, wiping them on his suit coat and tie. The tie was glossy black silk, patterned with tiny silver diamonds. A lovely tie, now yanked free of the neck, the knot as tight as an almond, bunched up in Vallance's fist.

"This young bloke who was going to invest," he began.

"What about him?"

"He told Allie a few things. Boasted about them."

"What things?"

Vallance smoothed the tie. Still his hands offended him. He

rubbed them on his thighs. "Understand that we'd decided we weren't going to have any more to do with him. I mean, this salvage thing is legitimate, I don't want some crim investing in it."

Gosse was interested. "He's a crim? What's his name?"

Chapter 35

As they drove west from the airport at Wynyard, something she said penetrated the recurring fog in Wyatt's head. "You tipped off CIB?"

"Yes."

"About me? About Raymond?"

Liz Redding wound down the window a little. "Some fresh air for your poor head. I said I tipped them off about Vallance."

"Oh."

"I saw Vallance and his lady friend with your nephew a couple of times. It didn't look right to me. I thought with Vallance removed from the scene, you and Raymond would abandon whatever it was you were up to. I wanted to save you from getting caught."

"Vallance had nothing to do with the paintings."

"I know that now. I didn't at the time."

There was Bass Strait on the right, a range of mountains on the left, but here the country was featureless, the kind of place where you nodded at the wheel and your speed crept up to 130,

140. Liz, Wyatt noticed, was driving at the limit, her eyes flickering between the road ahead and the rearview mirrors. She didn't once look at him.

"How do you know about Vallance?"

"I was attached to the Maritime Heritage Unit for a while. My job was to safeguard shipwreck sites from looters and track down looted goods. Vallance was working there, doing research, charting wrecks, that type of thing. He was given the sack. We couldn't prove anything, but we think he was stealing artifacts that were awaiting classification."

Wyatt was silent for a long time. He fished out the silver dollar that Raymond had given him. "Artifacts like this?"

Liz slowed the car, pulled on to the shoulder of the road. A semitrailer-load of wood ploughed past, storming the little rental car with a gust of wind.

"Let me see."

She turned the coin over and over in her slender fingers. "Did Vallance give you this?"

"He gave it to Raymond, Raymond gave it to me."

"Did he say where it came from?"

Wyatt said wearily, "Apparently from a wrecked ship called the *Eliza Dean*. Vallance had found the ship. It was carrying garrison pay to Hobart when it went down some time in the late eighteen twenties. Raymond went out to the site with Vallance. Said he saw coins just lying on the seabed."

Liz shook her head. "I remember when Vallance found that ship. He really did find it, it does exist, but there was never any garrison pay. A cargo of timber and sheep, from memory. It's not an important site. It's tucked out of the way and not even scuba divers or looters are interested."

Wyatt was putting a picture together in his head. "This coin—could it have come from another shipwreck?"

"Yes."

"It could be one of the things Vallance stole from the Heritage Unit?"

"Yes."

Wyatt took the coin from her fingers. A traffic policeman slowed, stopped adjacent to them, but nodded and sped off when Liz smiled and waved a road map at him.

"We'd better move on," she said.

"This is a Spanish dollar, right?"

"On its own it's proof that Vallance was lying to Raymond about the *Eliza Dean*," Liz said.

"How?"

"In eighteen thirteen the English government shipped forty thousand Spanish dollar coins to New South Wales. The Governor knew they wouldn't last, there was a coin shortage, so he stamped out the center portion of each Spanish dollar and created two coins from one. The holey dollar, and a coin of lesser value called a dump."

"I know all this."

"What you may not know is that by the eighteen twenties the coin shortage was over and in eighteen twenty-five the British government passed a law that only English sterling currency could be legal tender in the colony—two years before the *Eliza Dean* was sunk. Foreign coins, holey dollars, and dumps were recalled from circulation. That coin you've got there is unlikely to have come from the *Eliza Dean*."

"So what about the coins Raymond saw?"

"Vallance must have dived ahead of Raymond and salted the wreck. It's a not uncommon scam in the Caribbean, involving Spanish Main vessels."

"Salted" was an unfamiliar term to Wyatt but he guessed what Liz Redding meant by it. There was no treasure on the *Eliza*

Dean. Vallance had stolen old coins and scattered them near the wreck in order to attract cash investors, and Raymond had fallen for it.

He groaned. "Bloody fool."

"Raymond?"

"Yes."

"What will happen when he finds out?"

Wyatt shrugged. "Right now he's probably desperate because he doesn't have the cash he promised Vallance, and Chaffey is unlikely to give him any. He probably thinks he can use the paintings to buy into Vallance's syndicate, but if Vallance's under arrest and Raymond can't find him, he could do anything."

"You think Raymond's in danger?"

Wyatt said, "He was in danger from the moment he was born."

"How do you mean?"

"Look at the family he was born into."

"You're being too hard on yourself. He had choices."

Wyatt thought about Raymond's choices: Whether he should burgle houses or steal cars. Whether or not he should betray his uncle. Whether he should shoot Denise Meickle or slap her face to shut her up.

"Wyatt, will he come after you?"

Wyatt said, "I would put money on it."

Chapter 36

It was an odd sensation, knowing that she was in the house. Wyatt went for a prowl of the creek and nearby gullies and trees, tracing in his mind the useful landmarks: traps, places where they could hide, places of ambush. All the while he felt the pull of her, back there in his house.

When Wyatt walked back through his door a wall of heat enveloped him. Coals glowed in the open grate and freshly split logs had been tumbled onto the hearth. He looked around. He was not an untidy man, so he'd not left much that needed attention, but it was clear to him, from the aligned edges of an old newspaper and footprints showing against the raised weave of the carpet, that Liz Redding had cleaned and vacuumed the house.

Finally, as he advanced on the open fire, Wyatt made a swift appraisal of Liz herself. She was sprawled in an armchair, looking well-scrubbed and serene in a black tracksuit, with thick socks on her feet, her hair bright in the firelight, alive with static electricity. A cup and saucer on the end of the hearth held the dregs of weak black tea. He bent to kiss her.

Her cheek was cool. She made a sound in her throat. But, as he straightened, her composure cracked a little. She shifted self-consciously in the armchair, as though aware that she'd created a warm domestic cocoon but was in fact far from home and far from secure.

She turned away, fixed her gaze on the grate. Wyatt crossed to an ancient sideboard and cracked the seal on a bottle of Scotch. He poured a couple of fingers into a glass and left it on the mantelpiece while he swung the two-seater sofa to the opposite side of the hearth. But he stumbled, the room yawed, the sofa tipped with him to the floor.

All he wanted to do was lie there, in warmth and security, until the buzz and fog was gone from his head, but Liz was cupping his face in her warm hands. "You shouldn't make sudden movements. Do you want a doctor?" Her palms tensed. She began to slap his cheeks. "Wake up!"

Wyatt rolled onto his side, levered himself to his feet and righted the sofa. He collapsed into it, then remembered his Scotch.

Liz pushed him back. "Stay there. I'll get it."

Wyatt let the Scotch burn him into a state of relief from his trials. Liz, hovering uncertainly, sank into her armchair when she saw him smile thinly at her, saw the vulnerability rather than the customary chill in his hooded eyes.

She stared at his head. "You need a doctor." When he didn't respond she sighed. "At least get some rest."

"Right."

After a while she said, a little sadly, "I can't see you wanting me here with you."

Wyatt said nothing. Beyond sleep, he didn't know what he

wanted. He felt secure and warm, another chapter over. Then, as the Scotch burned a little more, the thought came unbidden into his head that he did want her there.

Then he felt her sit beside him, her thigh warm against his. In the light and warmth of the fire, Wyatt shifted position on the sofa and saw that Liz was watching him. Surprised by desire, the intensity and suddenness of it, he hooked his hand behind her neck. She shuddered. When they fell to the carpet, they made a clawing kind of love, Wyatt giving and getting back, finding a deep relief.

But when it was over, so was the pleasure. Wyatt didn't know Liz Redding, nor she him. They had desire and regard for each other, and were both in flight from the law, but that wasn't enough yet. He realized from her face that she shared his detachment, his drawing away. Her sadness matched his own. When the feeling passed they moved to the bed together for sleep. Wyatt wondered if he would wake in the morning and find her gone.

That was sad, too.

But if she *was* there—if he hadn't driven her away or allowed her to feel that she must go—then he would have to find a way of saying that he wanted her to stay. He wondered how people did that. Did they state it baldly? That's how he normally communicated his feelings, but surely that wasn't enough?

She was still there when he awoke at four in the morning. Moonlight streamed into the house, so he didn't bother with lights. He padded naked to the kitchen, downed a glass of tap water and mused at the window. That probably saved his life, for he was gazing unfocusedly across the moon-drenched open ground and otherwise might not have detected a flicker at the far end of the belt of trees that screened the house from the road. It was slight, and it was not repeated, but although stealthy it was not the movement of an animal of the night.

Wyatt drew back from the window and moved swiftly back to the bedroom. He clamped his hand over Liz's mouth, watched as she woke, struggled and subsided, before he whispered, "We have visitors."

She heaved against his hand. He released her. "Who?" she demanded.

"Keep your voice down. I don't know if they're after you or after me. They're not showing themselves."

Somewhere nearby the house creaked. Wyatt hissed, "Get into the wardrobe."

Liz pushed the bedclothes away and slipped across the room. She didn't question or argue further, and Wyatt saw that she had dressed again while he'd been asleep.

He thought of his nakedness then and pulled on jeans, hiking boots and a cotton sweater. He kept a .38 revolver strapped to the underside of the bedframe, and hurriedly dropped to the floor now and reached in and retrieved it. After a moment's thought, he shoved spare pillows under the bedclothes to suggest sleeping forms and placed a dark handkerchief on one of the pillows at the head of the bed.

Wyatt wished that he'd had more time to imagine his house defensively. He knew how to *escape* from it—he had a mental map of the rooms, doors and windows, their positions and dimensions—but what he needed to know was how to *use* the house. He concentrated for a moment, identifying the areas where light, natural or artificial, didn't fully penetrate. There were several: between the door to the kitchen and the refrigerator, the space behind the couch . . .

He ran out of time. He heard a footfall in the hall outside the bedroom and he rolled across the carpet until he lay flush where the wall met the floor. From this position he put his weight on his stomach and elbows and trained the .38 at the open door.

That might have worked if the shooter had been careless. Wyatt willed him into the doorway, even into the room, but all he got was a glimpse of a barrel. He was up against an assault rifle and a man who was too careful to frame himself as a target. Wyatt saw the barrel appear, squeezed off a shot from his .38, then all hell broke loose and he found himself deafened by the stutter of automatic fire. But he'd seen a face in the muzzle flash. It was Steer who had come to get him, not Raymond.

Chapter 37

When Steer had stepped onto the steel deck of Quincy's boat and shouted "Freeze!" he had the satisfaction of watching Raymond spasm in fright, almost piss himself with it.

Then, a few hours later, he watched Raymond all doubled over with seasickness, and that was pretty satisfying, too. Not the ultimate satisfaction—that was still to come—but still pretty good.

The trawler had ploughed on into choppy seas. Steer could have taken Raymond out in Melbourne, a clear shot to the brainbox while the little shit was trying to get into Chaffey's house, but a neighbor had been pottering around in the garden next door and Steer had decided to tail Raymond instead, hoping he'd lead him to the uncle.

Instead, it was to a one-horse town on the coast and Quincy and Quincy's boat.

Raymond had got his nerve back pretty quickly after the "Freeze." He'd swallowed, screwed a look of relief and apology onto his face and said, "Steer? Tony? Jesus Christ, man, I thought you'd be out of the country by now. I mean, when you didn't come back, me and Denise—"

Steer had broken in calmly: "You and Denise what?"

"Well, we figured that was it, you'd decided to go it alone."

"Did you just?"

Raymond had swallowed again. Quincy stood off to one side, bleary, a fag in the corner of his mouth, holding a rope. He'd swung his head, trying to follow the conversation.

"Yep," Raymond said. "Denise was that upset. She thought, that's it, I'll never see him again, he's walked out on me."

"I got delayed," Steer said.

Raymond managed a laugh. "Good to know you're okay."

Steer had watched Raymond without expression for a few long seconds, wondering how the little shit would play it.

"She was upset?"

Raymond nodded vigorously. "I'll say. Inconsolable. In the end she just cleared out."

"Is that a fact?"

"Yeah. She knew she'd be arrested if she went home. Said something about dropping out of sight up north somewhere."

"You don't say?"

Raymond had found encouragement in Steer's indifference. He took charge. "Mate, you can't stick around here. Plus you're too late for that boat Chaffey had lined up for you. I don't know what to suggest."

"*This* is a boat," Steer said.

"Forgetting my manners," Raymond said. He indicated the other man. "This here's Quincy. It's his boat."

"Quincy."

"Like the TV show," the bleary captain said.

Raymond frowned, clearly puzzled by the reference, but Steer knew it. Reruns of *Quincy, M.E.* had always been popular in the places Steer had been—Long Bay gaol, Bathurst, Yatala. All those men hoping the medical examiner would find the killer yet also hoping they'd learn how to make a murder look like a suicide or an accident.

"How about it, Quince? This tub make it to New Zealand for my mate here?"

Quincy contrived to look cunning. "It'll cost him."

"No problem," Steer said. "In the meantime, where are you two off to?"

Raymond had zipped open a red Thomas Cook bag. "Take a gander at this."

Old coins and ingots, worn by the tides, encrusted with the sediments of the sea.

"This stuff comes from a wreck out on the Cornwall Islands. Quincy's taking me there. Let's hope we're not too late. You want to get in on the deal?"

As transparent as glass. Steer saw it from Raymond's perspective: distract Steer from the question of Denise *and* get him out on the high seas where it was two against one. "Sure," he said.

And now he was in the bow, getting on for three hours out of Westernport, his head tipped back slightly, sniffing the wind, while Quincy stood in the wheelhouse and Raymond chucked his guts out over the side.

From the alignment of the bow with the coastline and the still clouds on the horizon, Steer judged that Quincy had turned a few degrees to starboard. Quincy seemed incurious enough about everything; probably did a spot of illegal abalone diving or was paid to go out and pick up bales of cannabis from the odd ocean-going yacht, but no doubt some internal head-scratching was going on.

Steer looked back. The Victorian coastline was receding in the afternoon light. Ahead of them lay choppier water. It wasn't bad; Steer had seen worse in his time. According to Quincy, there were no gale warnings, no storms expected. It was just surface chop, but it had got young Raymond in the guts. Steer smiled again.

Quincy caught his eye and winked comically. Steer nodded. Quincy wasn't a man who shaved or wore fresh clothes. Steer had spent a lot of time in gaol, a lot of time in cramped conditions, and a man soon learnt to value cleanliness. There was little toleration for the inmate who didn't wash, didn't make an effort. Just as well Quincy was downwind, in his wheelhouse. Steer took in the man's greasy overalls and towelling cap, his fuckwit's eyes in a nest of wrinkles, and turned back to his contemplation of the sea and fate.

He supposed that the treasure would be a bonus—if there was any. It would top up his two hundred grand, which had still been sitting in Chaffey's safe, wonder of wonders. Steer had felt certain that it wouldn't have been there, given the rip-off that Chaffey and Raymond were working on Denise and himself.

At his elbow, Quincy said, "Wouldn't have a smoke on you by any chance?"

Steer gazed past him involuntarily to the wheelhouse.

"Oh don't worry about this old darling," Quincy said. "I've set a course and she'll more or less keep to it for the time being. I mean, what are we going to hit out here? An iceberg? Fucking nuclear warship?"

A gurgling cough started deep inside Quincy and Steer realized that the man was laughing. He recoiled, stepped back a couple of paces, but Quincy followed. Quincy was a crowder. That was another thing you soon learnt not to do in the places Steer had been. To stall the sailor, Steer got out his Stuyvesants.

"Ta muchly," Quincy said.

Where Steer came from, a complex pattern of human

intercourse revolved around cigarettes. It wasn't like being on the outside, where you simply walked into a shop and bought smokes and smoked them. In gaol they were an item of currency. You bartered with them, accumulated and bought favors with them. They soothed you when you burned inside. You didn't, on any account, offer them without expecting something back. Quincy, puffing contentedly now, wasn't to know that, but that didn't lessen Steer's contempt for the man.

"Your little mate's puking his guts up."

They gazed at Raymond, who lay on his side near the starboard safety rail, both arms around his head. *He must be wrung dry by now,* Steer thought.

"Is there calm water around the islands?"

Quincy said that there was.

"He'll be okay when we get there."

Quincy looked at the sky, the deck, a point past Steer's shoulder. "I don't want no funny business."

Steer looked at him. Did the man mean sex? Does he think Raymond and I have a thing for each other?

"I don't want no shipwreck inspector arseholes breathing down my neck."

"Right," Steer said.

"Not worth the aggravation, know what I mean? They could seize this boat, fine us, slap us in gaol. Not worth it."

"I understand," Steer said.

They watched as Raymond rolled onto his other side.

"There's a thin blue line between fossicking and scavenging."

"I guess there is."

"Anything you find belongs to the government, by rights."

Now Steer had a fix on him. Seabirds sideslipped above their heads and the air hummed with a heady, briny ozone freshness. It was good to be alive. "We'll cut you in," Steer said.

Quincy's whiskery face contorted into an expression of cunning. "Nice to know we're on the same wavelength. Those other bastards your mate was partners with were paying me by the hour, only they skipped, owing me six hundred bucks."

"What other bastards?"

"Your mate's partners," Quincy said.

"Where are they?"

"Scarpered, most probably. They didn't smell right to me."

They gazed at Raymond. "So we work something out, okay?" Quincy said. "I'll see you don't get disturbed. If anyone shows, I'll have a good story ready, fishing rods over the side, stuff like that. We split whatever you find, no questions asked."

"Fair enough," Steer said.

Moron.

Quincy went back to the wheelhouse. They butted on through the swell and eventually Steer lost interest in the sea and Raymond and Quincy. He went below, found a paperback, and stretched out with it on his bunk. Later he took a chart up to Quincy, breathed shallowly while Quincy indicated the location of the *Eliza Dean*.

They anchored late in the day in a sheltered cove on the eastern side of the main island in the Cornwall Group. Steer stared at the little land mass and thought it a fitting place for a wreck, for tragedy, for the end of the line. He saw eroded red stone peaks, ferns, a tidal river between prongs of granite, wind-stunted sheoaks, Cape Barren geese, a few muttonbirds, oystercatchers and sandpipers, bare shoreline rocks, even a fur seal. There was a chill in the air.

Raymond had hauled himself to his feet as Quincy maneuvered the boat through the reef. He clasped the rail, pale and blurry. "This it?"

"This is it."

Quincy had taken another Stuyvesant from Steer. He ground it into the deck and winked. "Over the yard arm, boys."

Raymond stared at him suspiciously.

"Time for a drink, son," Quincy said.

Raymond groaned. "Not for me."

Quincy turned to Steer. "How about you? Game for a swig of something?"

Steer shook his head. "I'll pass. You go on and have one."

"Don't mind if I do," said Quincy delicately, and he waited, and he waited.

Steer understood. "Sorry, didn't bring anything with me."

"Oh, mate," Quincy said. "First rule, a bottle for the captain."

"Didn't know I'd be sailing with you," Steer said. He moved off. He was tired of this joker. "I need the bathroom."

He went below. When he appeared on deck again he was carrying canvas carryalls from the house in Warrandyte. Raymond was leaning tiredly on the rail. Quincy was waving his arms about, giving Raymond a history lesson.

Steer unzipped one of the canvas cases and pulled out the stun gun. As described in the mail order catalogue, it fired a disabling jolt of electricity, useful for crowd control and subduing violent men and animals. Steer walked up to Quincy, fired it at his head, and saw him drop, stunned, into the icy sea.

Raymond's jaw sagged. "Jesus. Mate. Steady on."

"She's been found, Ray. You think I don't listen to the news?"

"Who's been found?"

"You thought you could knock Denise and get away with it? I mean, what do you take me for?"

"Denise? I put her on a bus—"

"What happened, you try to race her off and she turned you down?"

Raymond backed away, eyes wide in pure fright. "I didn't

kill her. She was, you know, suicidal. I came back one day and found her. Or maybe she was cleaning her gun and it went off. Anyway, I panicked and dug—"

"Or how about this," Steer said. "You and Chaffey cooked the whole thing up. Get rid of me, get rid of Denise, pocket my dough. Only it went wrong, I didn't come back to the house with you."

"I swear. Ask Chaffey. He—"

"Chaffey's dead in his basement." Steer grinned then, a glittering cold grin of arrogance and vigor. Raymond looked away.

"Hey, Raymond, why so long in the face? Forget Denise. You tell me where Wyatt is and we're quits."

Raymond turned, relieved. He started to blabber out an address in northern Tasmania, then said, "Mate, if you want to waste him, be my guest. What'd he do?"

Steer stroked his chin, let the stun gun hang loose at his side. "You would've been a gleam in your old man's eye at the time. Wyatt set up this job, an American base payroll near Saigon. We'd done it before. Spent weeks putting this one together, a real perfectionist. I couldn't see any holes in the job, but at the last minute he pulled out, said it felt wrong. So me and a couple of others done it. The MPs were waiting for us. A setup, clear as the nose on your face. He wanted me out of the way. I think he struck a deal with the MPs, something like that."

"Bastard."

Steer saw the heat of strong emotions rise in Raymond, as though the little shit shared his sense of betrayal. Raymond shook his head in disgust and said, "You reckon that's how come he's stayed out of gaol so long? He makes deals with cops?"

"Bank on it."

"Anyway he—"

"Anyway, this is for Denise," Steer said, and he zapped

Raymond three or four times, backing him up to the rail, propelling him over the side. Steer watched for a while. Like Quincy, Raymond drowned quietly, his limbs feeble in the darkening water, as though stirring molasses.

There was some daylight left. Steer stripped, climbed into a wet suit, and contemplated the bottom of the sea. He didn't find anything on the seabed, but among Raymond's things on board the boat he did find a red vinyl Thomas Cook bag and a PVC cylinder with a couple of paintings in it. He spent the night anchored in the calm waters inside the reef. At dawn the next morning he sailed through the gap and headed southwest, across Bass Strait to the northern coast of Tasmania.

Chapter 38

Wyatt fired again, snapping off a shot through the open door as he rolled toward it. For some reason, Steer was firing high, spraying the room, and there was something unprofessional about that.

And then he realized why. As ejected casings from the automatic rifle spun to the floor, Steer stumbled on them, his feet threatening to slide away beneath him. Wyatt kept firing, more wildly now to take advantage of Steer's carelessness.

But he was also counting. With one cartridge left in the cylinder, he stopped firing. He was listening now, and through all of his faulty senses he heard a door bang shut, heard footsteps boom on the verandah, then silence.

He lay there for a short time, trying to blink away the muzzle flash on his retina, swallowing to clear the ringing in his ears. Steer's presence here told him that Raymond was dead. He also knew that Steer would want to finish what he'd started. He had run, but probably to a safe place so that he could work out how to try again. The house was isolated, the target a man wanted by the law, so he had no reason to fear neighbors or that Wyatt would call the police.

But it didn't seem likely that Steer would try again before daybreak, not when he'd lost the advantage. Daylight was a different matter. Steer could move more freely then, shoot with greater certainty, place the house under siege.

Wyatt had no intention of allowing that to happen. He would let Steer know that he was the hunter now, even though he had only the patchy moonlight to work with.

He fumbled in the darkness for a box of cartridges, whispered "Stay there," at the wardrobe door, then hurried to the window, pushed open the insect screen, and dropped to the verandah. For a moment he clutched the railing, waited for a wave of dizziness to pass, then ran at a crouch to the corner of the verandah. He saw from the dewy grass that Steer had returned to the clump of blackwoods, peppermint gums, and manferns below the house.

Wyatt guessed that he was about a minute behind Steer. Yet he also had all the time in the world. It was 4:30, and in the two hours before daylight broke over northern Tasmania, Wyatt went on the offensive.

He began by letting Steer know that he was in pursuit. His boots thudded on the open ground; once among the trees, he tore through the undergrowth, his sleeves and trousers snagging on blackberry bushes. He drew ragged breaths. He shouted a couple of times.

And then he would freeze for ten minutes, letting the silence build, letting it work on Steer's nerves. Panic levels rise at night in the bush. You lose track of your quarry, lose track of your own position, yet—absurdly, given the darkness—you feel that you are under a spotlight, that all guns are trained on you. That's how Wyatt read the psychology of the man he was up against and he hoped for a careless rush through the trees, or wild shots, but Steer refused to be drawn. He didn't even slap himself against the swarming mosquitoes.

Wyatt sniffed the air, trying to pinpoint Steer by smell, but got nothing. Steer knew all that Wyatt knew about tracking and hunting. They had trained together as snipers, after all, and no sniper will let himself be betrayed by insect repellant, dry-cleaning fluid, tobacco, shampoo, soap, deodorant, aftershave, or any other chemical.

Wyatt tried to recreate his own odors. Sweat and tangled sheets and Liz Redding.

And in the act of recreating his past few hours he saw the bedroom again, saw the spray of automatic fire criss-crossing the bed and stitching the walls.

Stitching across the wardrobe door, across Liz Redding's lovely torso? He wished that he could remember. He started to reload the .38—but something was wrong. The spare cartridges: they wouldn't fit. In his haste he'd grabbed 9mm ammunition for his Browning. A chill crept over his skin.

He shook it off. He waited in perfect stillness, like a fox, thinking about his next move. His mind flicked down the years to his youth, the army, Steer, trying to focus on Steer's weak points. Reluctantly he admitted that Steer matched him. Steer's only weakness was that he was fixed on getting even with Wyatt, and that wasn't a weakness unless he let his feelings get in the way of his intellect. Wyatt's flickering thoughts brought him to the present again, to the shot-up bedroom, and it occurred to him that Steer had outfitted himself with the wrong weapon for a cat-and-mouse game.

Wyatt hated automatic weapons. They jammed, they were sensitive to dirt and knocks, they required no skill other than to pull the trigger. Steer had simply stood back from the door, extended the barrel into the room and fired. The natural kick of the weapon had done the rest. The bullets, spraying at the rate of thirty per second, had striped the room. It was an inefficient, noisy, careless way to kill someone, and it was the wrong weapon for a stalking game. Wyatt would have fired only once and it would have been a kill shot. He wondered if his .38, with one shot left in the chamber, was the right weapon. But it wasn't his only weapon. He had his hands and his head, after all.

His hands and his head. They were not as efficient as they could be. His hands were no good if his head gave way to blackouts.

He moved. He'd been still for long enough. The daylight was coming and he needed to blend with the trees and the grass and a variety of earthen colors. He drew closer toward the creek, startling a bandicoot. Once or twice he mistakenly snapped a twig or brushed against bark, but waited for several minutes before moving on again, hoping that Steer would dismiss the noise as a random one.

At the creek's edge he found wallaby and potoroo tracks in mud that was the consistency of axle grease. He scooped palmfuls of the mud over his jeans and sweater, daubed it onto his face, scalp and the backs of his hands. The clay seemed to bind itself to him like an outer skin. It would be slow to dry, slow to flake away. He finished with leaves and stalks of grass, distributing them over his body until he wore mud and flora like a kind of gillie suit, as if he were a Scottish poacher or gamekeeper, not a manhunter.

In full daylight, Wyatt began to hunt Steer. The creek wandered through a gully several kilometers long, here and there concealed by thickets of dense trees, bracken and manfern fronds but mostly running through a trench across open ground with sloping grassland for dairy cattle on either side. Starting at one end of the trees at the bottom of the slope below his house, Wyatt passed silently and swiftly to the other. Steer was no longer there.

At the western edge he stopped and peered through a fine, stubborn mist at the open ground, scanning quickly, not letting his eyes rest for long, for fear that he might miss spotting a movement or a shape that didn't belong there. The creek tumbled over stones; birds greeted the morning: a grey thrush, crescent honeyeaters, satin flycatchers.

As Wyatt saw it, Steer had three choices: to follow the creek across open ground to the next belt of trees; to head left or right up a grassy slope to either rim of the little gully, where he'd be among trees again and have a clear shot downhill; or somehow conceal himself and let Wyatt get ahead of him, so that he could become the hunter and Wyatt the quarry.

Wyatt investigated this last option first. The only shelter outside of the trees was a clump of bulrushes. Breaking cover at a run, he weaved until he reached it. He saw at a glance that Steer hadn't stopped here. The bulrushes sat undisturbed and there were no tracks in the mud.

He crouched and stared out across the grassland on either side of the creek. There were plenty of ways of playing this. He could wait, letting Steer make the moves, the mistakes. If he kept moving, on the other hand, he'd maintain the advantage and maybe rattle Steer. He'd broken cover to get to the bulrushes, something he'd rather not have done. But Steer hadn't fired. Did that mean Steer hadn't seen him? It could be that he was on high ground, keeping watch on several locations at once, meaning that his concentration was split. Wyatt would make Steer break cover if he could, but why should Steer want to do that? Much better to stage an ambush.

Wyatt guessed that Steer was either on the run now or intending to set a trap away from the creek. He peered at the ridge on either side. Steer was up there somewhere.

He returned to the shelter of a peppermint gum and began to

think his way into the soil. He crouched and looked along the grass, letting the slanting light of early morning tell him where Steer had been. After a while, he found the signs: a bruised grass stem; disturbed pebbles, their moisture-darkened undersides revealed to the light; a patch of bruised lichen on a rock.

Wyatt began to track Steer, out of the trees and parallel to the creek. He found more signs: an indentation where Steer had knelt briefly; tiny grains of soil pressed to the bottom of a dead leaf; the crust broken on a cow pat; finally a footprint, the heel deeper than the sole, indicating haste.

Wyatt tracked more surely and swiftly now. He began to listen and watch for larger signs such as quail disturbed from the grass, black cockatooos screeching from the treetops. It was clear that Steer had not climbed to the rim of the gully but was heading parallel to the creek, making for the next thicket of stringy-bark and blackwood. Wyatt noticed dark, kicked-up soil; the lighter underside of grass revealed among the darker surface that faces the sun. He encountered obstacles—a quartz reef, fallen logs, and a tributary of the creek—where he lost the trail and had to gauge how Steer would reason his way past. He'd find the trail again, press on, knowing that he couldn't afford to take short cuts or try outguessing Steer, for backtracking would waste precious time.

Fifty meters short of the next thicket, he came to a depression in the ground and saw that Steer had rested there. Something gleamed wetly. He bent to look. Blood spots. Was Steer wounded? Had he cut himself? Wyatt climbed out, preparing to follow Steer's tracks into the trees, and noticed that Steer had changed direction. He was heading up and out of the gully after all.

Wyatt thought it through. He was wasting time following Steer like this. Steer might keep running, he might stop and set a trap because he was wounded, but either way he'd be expecting

Wyatt to come in behind him. As Wyatt saw it, he had to get ahead of Steer and ambush him.

He broke cover and weaved along the creek toward the trees. He ran through them, dodging branches and leaping rotten logs, and found himself at a culvert on a muddy backroad. The road told him where he was. If he went right he'd eventually reach the coast highway. If he went left, he'd climb out of the gully to the top of the ridge somewhere behind his house. He knew he'd find Steer there. If Steer had come by vehicle, that would be there too.

Still running, Wyatt scrabbled through a fence and up the embankment to the road itself and followed it uphill. It was a road subject to poor water drainage, and he stumbled often on the deep red ruts and washaways. At the top the going was easier, and he came upon an old F100 ambulance parked under a screen of trees, low branches touching the roof. Wyatt watched, and when he was satisfied that the van was unoccupied, he ran to the glass in the rear doors and peered in. Empty but for a red vinyl bag and a PVC cylinder. *That* has come a long way, he thought. When he peered through the driver's window he saw torn wires around the ignition.

He straightened from the window, formulating an ambush. Steer would be hypercautious as he approached the van. He'd search the trees, then the interior of the van itself.

Suddenly Wyatt heard a footscrape, heard Steer slide free of the tangling branches down onto the van roof, swinging the assault rifle at him like a club. That explained Steer's failure to shoot. His clip was empty or the firing mechanism had jammed. Wyatt fired his last bullet uselessly at the sky as he thought these things, and then Steer's rifle smashed against his temple and compounded all the hurt and damage of the years.

Later, when he stirred again, blinking at the light and daring to move, he saw that the sun was high in the sky. He turned onto his side. After a while, he levered himself to a sitting position, letting the front wheel of the van hold him upright.

"Bang, bang," Steer said. "You're dead."

Wyatt waited for the tilting world to right itself. He felt too weak to stand. It occurred to him that this was how he might die one day, his backside in the dirt, at the hands of a man like Steer.

What was Steer waiting for? Did he want to spell out his grievances first? *Unprofessional*, Wyatt thought.

He blinked and focused. Steer was opposite him, almost his mirror image, seated on the ground, his back to a tree. He had Wyatt's empty .38 in his lap, and when he saw sharpening intelligence in Wyatt's eyes, he raised the .38 and pulled the trigger, once, twice, a third time, a series of dry clicks. "Bang, bang," he said, as if he'd been playing this game all through Wyatt's blackness, wanting him to wake up. "Bang, bang," he said. "You're dead," and he coughed blood and began to fall.

Wyatt watched. He saw Steer topple onto his side, stretch, arch his back, and apparently die. He'd been gut shot. The blood had seeped into his clothing, darkening a huge area around his waist. Wyatt wondered about that. He put it down to a lucky shot through the bedroom door. He felt tired. He heard whispering footfalls in the grass, possibly the wind, and lay himself on the damp, rotting leaves to wait for Liz Redding, or possibly sleep, to claim him.